WANDA MILLER

LOVING

Noah

A Winn Series

Fox House and the Fox House colophon are Registered Trademarks of Fox House Publishing

Contact: www.foxhousepublishing.com

Library of Congress Cataloging-in-Publication Data

Names. Miller, Wanda, author.

Title: Loving Noah

Description: First FoxHouse Publishing Edition. 1 Virginia: FoxHouse LLC, 2020

ISBN - Paperback: 979-8-9988717-0-2
ISBN - Hardcover: 979-8-9988717-1-9

ISBN- Ebook: 979-8-9988717-2-6

First Edition: February 2022

Contents

A Life of Violence

T he tip of James's knife caught the light, shining like a second sun in the dimly lit room.

The man seated across from him was still breathing, though James had made a considerable effort to change that. Afterward, he cleaned his hands in a tin sink, the scent of blood masked by lavender dish soap and cigarette smoke. Guzman's instructions were clear: a few broken knuckles could yield a new informant, while a few broken ribs would silence a snitch forever. James gazed at his reflection in the water-streaked mirror above the sink, noting the unremarkable features of his face, except for the scar under his left eye and his unyielding stare. As he stood there, the silence seemed to intensify, creating a dull ache behind his temples. His phone buzzed twice against the dented metal counter, displaying an unknown caller. James hesitated for a moment, feeling the surge of adrenaline that had kept him alive in the darkest moments of his life, before finally answering the call. The ringing echoed through the empty warehouse. "Come on, Rivera," he muttered, seeking the reassurance of a familiar voice on the other end. Finally, Agent Rivera's voice broke through the static, urgent and questioning. "James? Is it done?" Rivera's urgency sent a shiver down his spine, a stark reminder of the high stakes involved. "Not yet," James replied, keeping his voice steady. "I just completed a job for Guzman, but I need to discuss the intel I received. It's more significant than we initially thought." He could almost hear Rivera processing the implications of this newfound information, envisioning the agent analyzing the situation.

As he spoke, images of Nicole's face flashed in his mind—her determination, her vulnerability. The thought of her made his heart ache, a painful reminder of the life he longed for but felt was endlessly out of reach. "I need this to end, Rivera. I can't do this anymore," James confessed, the words spilling out before he could hold them back. There was a heavy pause on the line, and for a moment, all he could hear was the distant hum of the city outside, a world filled with life that felt impossibly far from his own dark reality. "We'll make it work, James. Just hold on a little longer," Rivera reassured him, igniting a flicker of hope in his chest. But deep down, James knew that hope came with a price, and he was prepared to pay it.

The next day, James found himself in the lavish entryway of Guzman's mansion. The air was heavy with the aroma of pricey cologne and something darker lurking underneath. Guzman, sitting behind a huge desk, looked at him with a predatory sparkle in his eyes. "James, my right-hand man," he started, his voice smooth as silk. "I have a special job for you—one that needs your unique skills."

James gulped, feeling a knot of unease settle in his stomach. "What's the job?" he asked, trying to hide his nervousness. Guzman leaned in, a twisted grin spreading across his face. "There's a journalist—Nicole Winn. She's been a pain in my side, and I need you to get into her IVF clinic. Swap her sperm donor with mine. I want to make sure she pays for making me look weak."

James's heart raced, a mix of disgust and fear washing over him. "You want me to mess with her family's future?" he asked, struggling to keep his voice steady. Guzman shrugged, unfazed. "Family is a tool, James. We use it to our advantage. Plus, you'll be doing me a favor. Once this is done, I'll have a new ace in our game."

James nodded, hiding his dread, but inside he was screaming. He stepped out of Guzman's office, feeling the weight of the world on his shoulders. The mansion was a maze of wealth and power, but it felt more like a prison made of glass and gold. Each step echoed with the realization that he was being drawn deeper into a web of manipulation and deceit.

As he walked down the long hallway, the fancy decor blurred into a haze. He saw Rodriguez leaning casually against a marble pillar, his eyes sharp and predatory. "You were in there for a while," Rodriguez said, the corners of his mouth twisting into a fake grin. "I hope Guzman wasn't asking too much of you. You know how he gets when things don't go his way."

James met Rodriguez's gaze, forcing himself to stay calm. "Just the usual business," he said, attempting to downplay the tension. But Rodriguez could see right through him, his smirk growing wider. "You ought to realize, James, that loyalty is crucial in our field. If you ever start doubting your role, it might be time to rethink your position."

The weight of his words lingered heavily in the air. James felt a surge of anger bubbling beneath the surface; he refused to let Rodriguez intimidate him. "I know my place," he shot back, infusing his voice with determination. "And you should keep that in mind."

Rodriguez raised an eyebrow, clearly amused by their back-and-forth. "We'll see how long that determination holds up. You have a knack for landing in hot water, and I'd hate for Guzman to think you're not capable of handling this." With that, he pushed off from the pillar and strolled away, leaving a sense of unease behind.

James inhaled deeply, trying to shake off the residual tension. He needed to concentrate on the task at hand, no matter how distasteful it felt. He had to gather intel on the clinic, figuring out how to infiltrate it without causing any alarms. As he stepped outside into the crisp night air, the weight of his decision pressed down on him again.

He pulled out his phone and dialed Agent Rivera's number, hoping to clarify the situation. As the call connected, James braced himself to discuss the details of his new assignment and seek advice on how to navigate this without losing himself.

"James? What's happening?" Rivera's voice came through, sharp and alert.

"I've got a lead on Guzman's next move," James responded, his voice steady yet tinged with urgency. "It involves a journalist, Nicole Winn. He wants me to sabotage her IVF procedure by switching the sperm donor."

There was a moment of silence on the other end, and James could hear Rivera thinking things over.

"That's a risky move, James. Are you really sure you want to go ahead with this? It could put you in a tough spot."

"Tough is putting it mildly. But if I don't see this through, I risk everything—not just for me, but for her and her family too." A knot twisted in his stomach at the thought of Nicole's face—her dreams for the future crushed by his choices.

"Take your time. We need to sort this out carefully," Rivera insisted. "This isn't just about taking Guzman down; you have to look out for yourself as well. If things go south, it could cost you your life."

James hung up, the weight of the situation hitting him hard. He felt like he was on the edge, balancing between his past and the life he was desperate to leave behind. With every second of doubt, he could hear Rodriguez's taunts ringing in his ears. He had to make a decision—a decision that could turn everything upside down.

Determined, he made his way to the car, the engine's roar igniting his determination. He couldn't let Rodriguez or Guzman control his destiny. As he drove toward the clinic, the night air whipped past him, a reminder that he was still alive—still capable of fighting for the future he wanted. With every mile, he braced himself for the challenges ahead, ready to confront the fallout of his choices head-on.

The clean smell of antiseptic hit James as he walked into Dr. Cross's office, his heart racing with a mix of excitement and nervousness. The walls were lined with framed diplomas and awards, each showcasing the doctor's skill in reproductive medicine. Yet, right now, the pressure of Guzman's task hung over him like a dark cloud.

"You know I could lose my job, right? My practice? I'd be ruined."

"I doubt your six-figure salary, along with what Guzman is paying you, would put you in financial crisis."

"Crisis? I'm talking about jail. I wouldn't last a day in a place like that." He gripped the plastic clipboard, thinking of this decision driven by greed.

"You know Guzman," James stared at the doctor, hoping to trigger some form of common sense as to who they were dealing with, and couldn't procrastinate the decision he was being threatened into.

"I know all too well what happens when you break promises with Mr. Guzman. There's still a missing persons case on the other doctor he was dealing with before me. I try not to think about it."

"Then you know he's serious about what he's asking you to do."

"It still doesn't make it right. This is morally and ethically wrong."

"She's caused Mr. Guzman to lose a lot of money due to her investigation into his businesses. He's got every right to protect his investments."

"Protect his investments? By stealing a pregnancy? It's one thing to help a young woman to become a mother, Mr. Williams. It's another thing to play God when it's not our place."

James lowered his head. "Believe me, Doctor Cross, this isn't the way I want things to happen. The child and the woman deserve better. But I have a job to do."

Dr. Cross nodded in acceptance of his fate. "Yes, I understand. Your job is more important than a woman's decision to raise a child without the threats of danger. If you will excuse me, my patient is in the waiting room on time for her appointment. Do make yourself inconspicuous while exiting my office."

James grabbed the doorknob. "Everyone has a job to do, Dr. Cross. I'm just here to make sure it gets done correctly."

He walked slowly down the hallway. The curious eyes following him but not asking for his name provoked a bit of irritation, but he kept going until he reached the waiting area.

That's when he saw her.

He stood there in silence watching her open a small laptop for a moment, just before leaving with a slight twinge of regret.

His job in this business was finished.

James sat anxiously waiting for the figure in the backseat to reveal himself. Guzman couldn't have sent one of his men to kill him. He must be here to see if James would make good on his promise of seeing the doctor to get the job done. He would've gone with that theory if the man hadn't pulled out a knife, going for the center of his chest.

So much for loyalty.

James spun around suddenly, grabbing the knife with his left hand before elbowing the killer in his face several times. The man's eyes went from watery chest-nut to a wicked brown as the fight intensified. He was dazed seconds before lunging again with the knife but was caught by the wrist, and with a quick snap, his cries could be heard echoing in the garage parking lot.

"Fuck you!" The man held his dangly wrist as James aimed his gun.

"Is that what you told Guzman before he sent you to come after me? Or was it, 'Yes, Boss, consider it done"?

The man attempted to calm his breathing as it escaped in quick bursts. James steadied his finger on the trigger and yelled, "Answer me!"

The man spat out a mouthful of blood. "You're dead. Just remember I had the balls to say it to your face."

He needed to hear the words first. The moment of clarity was absolute for him but detrimental for his would-be killer. These would be his last words on this earth. Bullets exited the chamber in three shots, lodging themselves inside the killer's chest.

He slammed the car door, his insides a haze of rage and betrayal. Guzman had turned on him. He snatched his phone out, thumb hovering over the call button, when a thought pushed its way into his mind like an intruder in the night. A grin of pure defiance spread across his face.

He didn't want to just betray James; he wanted him gone. But what if the ultimate betrayal was turning the tables? Guzman's legacy could become James's own seed. He shoved the phone back in his pocket and sprinted toward the building, leaving behind the dead man's body, slumped and leaking its life out onto the leather seats.

James burst into Doctor Cross's office, breathless and electric with a new purpose.

"It's happening," he announced. "But my way."

The doctor barely looked up from his clipboard, dark circles nesting beneath his eyes. "What do you mean?"

"Forget Guzman," James said. "Use my sperm."

Across from him, Dr. Cross offers a nod of acceptance after James tells him his plan. "Mr. Williams, are you sure about this?" The question cuts through the air, unsettling the silence, as James follows him in with a gait more determined than the moment allows.

Doctor Cross adjusts his glasses, thin metal frames catching the light. "You know," he says, his voice uncolored by emotion, "most of our clients don't make this kind of arrangement."

James leans forward, a deliberate move that anchors him to the room's stark reality. "Most of your clients aren't me," he replies, his voice low and controlled. He sees the doctor register his resolve, a clinical curiosity crossing the man's features.

Cross set the clipboard down and rubbed his temples. "Do you understand what you're doing?"

"More than you think," James said, leaning over the desk, needing this man to see the fire in his eyes. "I'm taking back my life."

There was a pause as Cross weighed the situation, each second a brick added to the wall of tension between them. Finally, he nodded slowly. "Okay. We'll proceed with what we have. But do you know the risks?"

"The risk is doing it his way. This is how I win." James stood still now, resolute as a statue, the anger in his eyes cooling into something more focused, something dangerous.

Cross nodded again, resigned but compliant. "We'll begin immediately then."

He keeps his hands clasped, fingers twitching against the echo of old reflexes, ready for more action even in this unnaturally still place.

The air is sharp with disinfectant and a silence that expects to be filled. James finally speaks, the words as sharp as the scalpel he imagines in the doctor's hand. "When the time is right—in ten years—make sure that kid knows who I am." It's a command wrapped in hope, a lifeline he's throwing into the future.

The doctor studies him for a moment longer, then nods, making a note on his tablet. "That's a long time, Mr. Williams," he says. "Things can change."

"Things always change," James answers, a flicker of something like sadness playing across his otherwise steady gaze. "But I need your assurance that this won't."

The doctor leans back, a smooth movement that suggests neither reluctance nor eagerness, only the weight of his profession. "We'll document it, as you've requested. And in ten years—" His voice trails off, letting the enormity of the commitment speak for itself.

James imagines a decade stretching out before him, the child growing with each turn of the calendar, unaware of the history written into its genes. He pictures himself in the waiting and the risk that the distance of time might also be the distance of memory. "It's important," he says, pushing the gravity of his need into every syllable.

"May I ask why?" The question is devoid of the personal interest it implies, the doctor's curiosity tempered by the boundaries of his role.

James pauses, his eyes narrowing slightly as if focusing on an invisible horizon. The explanation is there, tangled with so much he cannot untangle, so he offers only the parts he can. "It's complicated," he finally says, leaving the word hanging like an unlit match in the sterile air.

"Everything is," the doctor replies, a slight smile touching his lips before it fades into the same professionalism that saturates the room. He scribbles something more on the tablet, the pen moving like an instrument of finality.

"You'll be notified, of course, if anything changes," the doctor finally says, rising with the same efficiency that has defined their meeting. "And in ten years, if all goes as planned—" He doesn't need to finish; the words linger between them like an oath, a tenuous promise waiting to be kept.

James stands, the fluid motion of a man accustomed to executing precise decisions in a world less controllable than his own. "I appreciate it," he says, each word a quiet testament to the enormity of his ask.

The doctor extends a hand, their shake as brief and professional as the meeting itself. "We'll be in touch, Mr. Williams."

James leaves the room with a pace as steady as the ticking seconds, his mind echoing with the choice he's just cemented. In the hall, the white glare of the lights follows him, a witness to both his resolve and his uncertainty.

Outside, the world resumes its familiar chaos, horns blaring and engines rumbling as they push against the clinic's isolated silence. He pauses at the curb, the antiseptic air of the place still clinging to him like a second skin, a reminder of the promise that now ties him to an unwritten future.

That same traffic light that led him into the garage of Doctor Cross' office was taking forever to turn green to lead him out. It didn't matter that he had a dead body in the back seat or swapped his sperm in place of Guzman's at the office. What mattered was his instructions for the child he impacted. That one day, if he or she chose to find him, his residence would be a Maryland address. His hands hit the wheel several times. Dammit. All it took was Doctor Cross to reveal what he'd done, and this whole thing would blow up. He had gambled with a known killer and left that office with loose ends. But he knew Cross wouldn't turn him in? That look of disgust when he mentioned his plan minutes before he went in to perform the procedure was all the confirmation he needed; the good doctor was on board.

Nicole sat on the bed with her feet dangling against the soft linens. She daydreamed about holding her infant child for the first time, about buying tiny clothes at the mall, and about unexpected morning kisses when she would least expect them; all these things seemed so real now that she got the job at Maryland's top newspaper.

"Mrs. Winn?"

"Yes," she said dreamily. "Oh, hello, Doctor Cross.

"Are we ready?" He seemed nervous to her, a bit rushed. She brushed it off; one had to be a little nervous doing a procedure that costs six thousand a pop.

"Yes, I'm ready."

"Good. Now after this embryo transfer, you will be given a pregnancy test. Did the nurse explain this to you?"

"Yes," she said, "the process usually takes around 4 weeks."

"That's correct. So, I don't want you to worry. Everything looks good. Go about your daily lives, and we'll reconvene at your next appointment."

The procedure took less than ten minutes.

"Thank you, Doctor Cross."

"You are most welcome. Lie here for another fifteen minutes, and then you're all set to go."

The door closed quietly behind him, leaving her alone again to her thoughts; however, this time she was excited for the little person that would be growing inside of her. The next nine months were sure to be an exciting time.

Nicole put her clothes back on and headed towards the exit. She looked forward to her next appointment because that appointment could confirm her pregnancy. Her phone rang just as she was getting into her car. "I can't talk right now, Mom; Dad's words were clear enough. I really expected some form of acceptance, but I was wrong."

"Your father is right beside me, Nic, and would like to talk with you." She heard the phone being shoved back and forth with grumblings in the background. He was still being stubborn, and she didn't need more of his negative words when it came to her marriage. "Mom, put me on speaker."

"Alright, you're on speaker. We all can hear one another."

"In four weeks, you'll know if you have another grandchild on the way. What do you think about that, Dad?"

The communication was silent until her father finally broke his silence. It was finally time for the major to apologize to his middle daughter.

"Nicole. I just want what's best for you, and I'm sorry for the things I've said. I was wrong. Forgive me, please..."

His voice trailed off, finally an emotion from him that she could recognize.

"When can we visit Nic?" Her mother's voice was anxious; she needed closure from this feud as well.

Nicole held back emotional tears. "How about tomorrow, dinner?"

"Tomorrow sounds good," she said in an elated voice. "We love you, Nic." The last sentence she heard before the phone hung up.

"Tomorrow sounds perfect."

Father Figure

1 0 years later

Noah played with the zipper on his backpack, trying to forget how small he felt. Above him,
big blue letters said Baltimore Family Fertility Services,
and posters promised happy families because of mod-
ern science. Below, couples sat in soft chairs, looking at
him with awkward stares before quickly looking away.
Noah's eyes were fixed on the reception desk. A nurse in
a neat white blouse looked at the paper in his hand, then
nodded and leaned in to listen.

Noah held the page tightly; it was a copy of his
mother's clinic files. It had words he hadn't seen until recently: artificial insemination, biological father, anonymous. He stared at the files again, hoping the words
would change, remembering how they had been on the
kitchen table weeks ago when his mother thought he was
asleep. He could hear adults talking softly in the wait-

ing area. An older couple nearby nudged each other to look at him. When Noah glanced their way, they quickly turned, pretending to look at the carpet instead.

Noah took a deep breath and walked up to the desk, feeling nervous in his stomach. He knew the couple was watching him, but he was more worried about his mom's, Nicole and Renée, who could walk in any moment. That thought made him hurry. He reached the reception area and held onto the counter, his fingers leaving smudges on its shiny white surface. A small plant was almost tipping over the edge. He leaned in, trying to speak quietly without drawing attention.

"Can you help me?" he whispered, his voice barely heard over the chatter.

The nurse, named Julie, paused her typing. She looked from Noah to the paper he was holding and back. Seeing a child alone in a room full of adults made her look concerned but kind. Noah shifted his weight, feeling tense.

"Well, aren't you brave?" Julie said, pulling out a small notebook. "What do you need, sweetie?"

He swallowed and glanced back to make sure the entrance was clear. "There's a name we don't have in the files. I need to know who he is."

The nurse tilted her head, looking sympathetic. Noah noticed the woman across the room nudging her husband again, which caught his attention. He turned away and focused on the nurse's hand holding the pencil.

"Can you write down the name and address?" he asked, his voice a bit stronger but still quiet.

Julie nodded slowly, showing that she understood more than he had said. "Let me get this for you." She wrote something on a notepad, tore off the page, and looked between the door and Noah's serious face.

Noah watched her closely, his fingers running along the edges of the files.

Julie leaned over the counter and handed him the paper. "This should help. Just remember to talk to your moms about it, okay?" Her gentle words stung more than Noah expected.

He nodded, too focused on what he had to do to worry about promises he might not keep. The address on the paper was clear, and the name next to it made his heart race: Williams, James. "I'll send him a letter today," Noah said, saying the name out loud to remember it better.

Julie looked at him carefully. "You take care now," she said, mixing kindness and a hint of warning in her voice.

Holding the paper and files tightly, Noah stepped back from the desk. He briefly met the eyes of an older couple, and this time, they smiled as if they shared a secret he had just discovered.

He walked toward the exit, quickening his pace as he looked around the room. Even the simple posters—Successful Families Start Here—seemed to know where he was going. The farther he got from the clinic, the easier it was to breathe. With every step, his determination grew, and he thought about what James would be like and what it meant that he existed.

The door chimed as he opened it, and the cool air outside felt refreshing. He paused to glance at the clock above the reception desk. The bright red numbers read: 4:28. He left the building and its awkward stares behind, ready to discover the parts of his story he hadn't known were missing.

James expected a brief introduction and then a quick exit. On a crisp fall Saturday afternoon in Rockville, Maryland, his white pickup truck pulled into a parking spot beside a superhero birthday sign pointing in one direction. The truck's presence sharply contrasted with the line of minivans and smaller cars parked along the street. In James's pocket, the folded envelope felt as heavy as a stone, laden with significant implications. Before him, the Winns' brownstone rose, its front steps leading toward a future he believed could be his.

He noticed a tiny pair of eyes observing him from behind the blinds of the two-story house. Finally, he would meet the child that had written the letter to him.

Noah was dressed in his best sports outfit with matching sneakers. He watched intently as the man surveyed the house with a serious expression, then put on a blue sports coat and adjusted its collar. Standing at the window, Noah waited, his eyes never straying from the man before him.

James Williams stepped forward wearing a crisp white shirt that accentuated his ebony skin, his stylish fade, and his deep coffee-brown eyes. His blue jeans, outlining his thick, muscular thighs, caught his attention as he brushed off lint, glanced at his watch, and stared at the front door. At thirty-five, his single life had been moving along in a lonely, predictable way until a letter arrived in his mailbox, demanding he attend his son's birthday party. One of the top consultants for Wolf Pack Securities, with a Potomac house and a two-car garage, James's previous job had left little room for relationships or family visits—aside from the occasional trip to his parents' farm in Ashland, North Carolina.

Taking a deep breath, he knocked on the door.

The sound of the door lock rattling was quickly followed by it swinging open, revealing a boy around ten years old, a near mirror image of a younger version of himself. "You must be James?" the boy inquired, deliberately steadying his voice.

"As calmly as possible," James replied, "I received a letter saying there was a birthday party, and I should attend." Is that right?"

"Yeah, that's right. I sent it," the little boy said, shuffling his feet and offering a half-smile—a smile he had practiced in front of the mirror a week earlier, though the words had somehow never fully escaped his lips.

Then, with tentative hope, the boy asked, "Are you... my dad?"

"I think so," James answered softly.

Anyone who saw them together would recognize them as father and son—they were practically carbon copies, save for the amber eyes the boy had evidently inherited from his mother, a trait absent on James's side of the family. Noah had his father's facial features, coal-black hair, and a set of soon-to-be-broad shoulders.

"Where's your mom? May I speak with her?" James inquired.

"Come in. Both of my moms are out back," Noah answered quickly, spinning and bolting down the corridor.

"Moms?" The word reverberated in James's mind like a forbidden secret. Following the boy through the threshold into the main living area, James braced himself for the storm of emotions. He had imagined the enigmatic woman he'd once encountered a decade ago at Doctor Cross's clinic. His heart pounded as memories surged—a woman who had haunted his dreams, a phantom he had obsessively monitored from afar, always wondering if she was receiving the care she deserved. Always a safe distance, he'd watched from shadows, desperate yet terrified to pry. And now, fate thrust him face-to-face with the past.

He found her deep in conversation with an older man who seemed oddly out of place amid the casual party décor. Dressed in an elegant Italian suit with carefully combed hair, the man exuded a hint of professionalism that set off James's suspicions, compelling him to watch their interaction intently. The woman, standing on a small footstool to reach his eye level, appeared completely oblivious to James's arrival. In an almost instinctual motion, Noah nearly collided with her before turning slightly and mouthing, "This is Mom."

"Noah, stop running through the living room, please! What have we said about running in the house?" Her voice rang out like a whip, laced with exasperation as she tried to corral the whirlwind that was her son, darting toward the party.

James observed her exasperated sigh as she attached a streamer to the outer door frame. With her hair pulled back in a ponytail and her face natural and free of makeup, she looked stunning—like someone fresh off the cover of a DIY magazine, her white tank top accentuating a copper-toned upper body paired with blue jeans. Instantly, he felt drawn to her.

Their conversation resumed briskly.

"I'm done wasting time with your office attorney, Givens. If I need to uncover anything, I'll do it myself. Thank you," she declared.

"Mrs. Winn, you've repeatedly asked my office to examine allegations against our police department regarding drug activities, and I have yet to find anything incriminating," the man replied calmly.

"Maybe you're just not digging deep enough. The district attorney's office should have produced a comprehensive report on every bit of illegal police behavior by now, yet every lead gets ignored—or worse, someone vanishes. Why is that?" Her voice escalated with fury.

The man shook his head and turned to leave, only to notice James standing nearby, curiosity evident in his posture.

"Be careful, Mrs. Winn. These matters have a way of trapping even the most well-intentioned people. If you need me, you know where to find me," he added with a nod toward James before departing.

James had hoped the woman would acknowledge him, but she remained focused on pinning the decorations to the doorframe. Clearing his throat until her eyes met his, he said, "I'm sorry to intrude. My name is James Williams."

Nicole looked up at him, noting how his commanding frame filled the space between the couch and the doorway. It wasn't merely his proximity that unnerved her—it was the way he looked at her, as if studying every detail. After a brief, awkward silence, she spoke, "Hi, James. Are you with the superhero troupe? You can change in the guest house; a couple of guys are already setting up out there."

He offered a nervous laugh. "No, I'm not with the superheroes. Noah invited me. I'm his biological father."

The weight of that confession nearly toppled her, but before she could falter, two strong, steady hands encircled her waist and guided her gently to stand. How had he moved so quickly? Their eyes met again, charged and searching. Nicole marveled at the paradox—his hands, capable of both overwhelming strength and tender care. As he steadied her on the polished wood floor, he seemed to momentarily suspend time.

"What did you say?" Nicole managed to ask as she broke the brief connection. Her breath came in quick, uneven waves as she fought to regain composure. Could this be some sort of cruel joke? His firmly earnest expression suggested otherwise. Crossing her arms defensively, she thought only someone with pizza stains on their freshly bought shirt playing in the backyard could explain this situation.

"I assume he didn't tell you?" James said softly.

"No, he didn't," she replied as she half-turned toward the back door.

"Renée, can you come in, please?" Nicole called out.

Earlier that week, she had sensed Noah's distant mood but had let him be, believing he'd confide in her when the time was right. An open, honest relationship with her son was something she fiercely guarded—especially now, with a man named James claiming to be his father.

Renée appeared in the doorway, an apron and a bowl of popcorn in hand, her voice cheerful despite the turbulence. "It's almost two o'clock! Are the superheroes ready yet?"

"Renée, this is James. Noah invited him to his birthday party."

The silent shock hung heavy in the room as James cleared his throat and extended his hand, attempting to master his inner storm before facing more prying questions about his true purpose in their midst.

Renée's handshake was firm as she quickly bombarded him with questions. "So, Noah invited you? How do you know our Noah?"

"This is Noah's biological father."

"I'm his biological father." The declaration forced out simultaneously by both, leaving a buzzing void of stunned silence. Renée's wide eyes flitted between Nicole and James. With a resigned sigh, she removed her apron and set it aside, leaving the room filled with nothing but the echoes of distant children's laughter and the palpable weight of awkward uncertainty. They all stood like lifeless marionettes in a grim tableau until Renée decisively broke the silence.

"We need to sit down and talk."

At just ten years old, Noah was already displaying impressive detective skills, growing into a handsome, bold, and curious young boy. His search had begun at age five; every unanswered question about his origin only fueled his curiosity further.

From that day forward, a palpable tension blanketed the house as Noah's desire to learn about his biological father intensified. Aware that he was not yet ready, Renée and Nicole agreed to delay any serious discussion of his paternity until he was mature enough to understand. Yet, their pleas for him to drop the subject always fell on deaf ears—he would simply ask more questions. Renée tried to reassure them that Noah would eventually outgrow this fixation, and she was determined to change the subject whenever it arose.

Just a month earlier, a heated backyard discussion about Noah's biological father had ended abruptly when they realized neighbors had gathered to listen. Embarrassed, they had all retreated inside the house, avoiding the inevitable confrontation that might up-end their lives. Noah, however, was insistent on having a father figure who could engage with him in ways his mother couldn't, even though Nicole tried bonding through sports and other traditionally masculine activities. Baseball served as his outlet, allowing him an escape in the batting cage when Nicole joined him. Despite challenges like a volatile temper, peer pressure, and the growing pains of having two moms, at least their extended family offered a degree of support.

Nicole's parents had initially reacted poorly when their youngest daughter revealed she was a lesbian. Disapproval reigned, with her mother frequently shifting the subject out of discomfort and her father even attempting to set her up with neighborhood men—firm in his belief that only a traditional marriage would do. He viewed Nicole as the rebellious outlier who defied his conventional vision of a family.

The news of Nicole's marriage ignited a fierce argument, forcing both sides to distance themselves until tensions eased. Eventually, Nicole's pregnancy broke the ice; her parents welcomed her and her spouse with open arms. Nicole's father even apologized, admitting he had been an "asshole" and promising never to question her choices again. Nicole was grateful to see him come to respect her decisions and cherish his new grandson.

Eager to bond with his grandson, Nicole's father compiled an endless list of activities—from fishing and bowling to playing checkers—hoping to make up for past neglect. At the slightest sign of distress, Noah would be scooped up in his doting grandfather's arms and carried inside. Nicole's parents showered him with toys and food, and they assured her that their home was always available when Nicole and Renée needed a break. Yet, their hard-won family harmony was occasionally marred by the overt discrimination of neighbors, whose disdain appeared in community app messages and cold stares at homeowners' association meetings. While Nicole and Renée could tolerate minor challenges, outright harassment was unacceptable.

Renée studied James as he sat across from them. Immediately, she saw the resemblance—he was a handsome, older version of Noah, with the same brown skin, a square chin, and a quietly commanding masculinity. His eyes exuded warmth as they flitted between Renée and Nicole, occasionally lingering inappropriately. Scratching his head, he shifted his focus to the family photos on the table, smiling fondly at images of baby Noah as he leaned in closer. Midway through, his gaze met Nicole's, much to Renée's irritation.

"Wow, it's like looking at my twin..." he murmured.

But Renée interrupted, "The contract clearly stipulates zero contact with the sperm donor. So, how did you get our information?"

He replied, "That's exactly how I understood it, too. And please, just call me James—'sperm donor' doesn't sound appealing."

"I'm sorry. This is all very new to me, to us. It's unsettling," she admitted.

"When I received the letter, I felt equally strange. I've never experienced anything like this before."

"May I ask how many times you've donated to couples like us?" Nicole pressed.

"This is my first time donating. I thought giving someone a child would be a great contribution, but it seems to have caused more confusion than clarity."

"Renée, could you call Noah in here, please? He has a lot of explaining to do."

Renée quickly walked to the patio door and closed it firmly behind her. Turning to Nicole, James said, "I want you to know I feel uncomfortable too. I'm sorry if my presence has ruined your day," he said, trying to ease her evident anxiety. Nicole nodded, her stomach churning with unresolved emotions. Something about this man unsettled her.

Returning to the living room, Renée said a quick prayer and squeezed Noah's arm reassuringly. The boy hesitated, aware that the gathered adults were disappointed and might stifle his confession; his feet dragged until he was standing before his parents.

"Noah, can you tell us why Mr. Williams is here, please?" Renée asked.

"Start from the beginning, and don't leave anything out," Nicole urged.

Noah's legs wobbled as he began. "I just wanted to know who my father was. All the other kids at school have dads to play baseball and football with, and I got curious. So, I saw a letter in the mailbox and called the number on the paper. A nurse helped me."

"Letter in the mailbox?" Nicole asked.

Someone had to help because the donor isn't listed in our file, but with the clinic's donor record, his name should be there," Renée countered.

Noah continued, "The nurse was really kind. She wrote James Williams's name and address for me."

"Noah, do you realize what you've done? You've compromised someone's job and our trust. How could you go through our things?" Nicole scolded,

"Are you going to tattle on Nurse Julie? She was only trying to help me."

"I think you need to go to your room for the rest of the day."

"But all my friends are outside," Noah protested.

Before anyone could respond further, James interjected, "May I talk to Noah for just a minute?"

Nicole covered her face in frustration, knowing that more would have to be addressed concerning Nurse Julie—but for now, everyone needed to cool off. "Yes, that will be fine. Renée, can we speak privately in the room, please?"

Once out of Noah's earshot, Nicole turned to Renée and asked, "What do you think about all this?"

Renée's response was measured: "It might be a good thing."

"How's that?"

"Think about it—James might teach him things we can't. He could connect with Noah in ways we wouldn't even fathom."

"I'm scared he might take him away from us," Nicole whispered, the fear and uncertainty raw in her tone.

"Nicole, are you afraid of him connecting with Noah or of losing him entirely?"

"Both! We don't know him at all. What if he's a serial killer, or worse—a psycho who harms kids?"

"Nicole, seriously. I didn't get those vibes. I sensed he's as curious about Noah as Noah is about him. I don't believe he traveled all this distance to cause harm."

"I just can't trust that we know nothing about him," Nicole countered desperately.

"No, we don't fully know him yet. Let's try another angle." Renée turned Nicole around, directing her gaze towards the scene of James and Noah engaged in quiet conversation.

Nicole exhaled slowly, the tension releasing in a fragile surrender. "Our son is happier than I've ever seen him since starting school. Let's give Mr. Williams a chance and decide together if this is truly the best thing for Noah."

Nicole's investigative skills as a seasoned journalist, honed by probing high-profile stories, meant that digging into James's background was yet another task to add to her already heavy workload. She was in the midst of covering the opioid crisis in Bay Ridge County and an exposé on flaws within the local police department. Fresh off a celebrated series on the disappearance of Black women in Maryland—a series that had earned her team prestigious accolades—she was determined to keep the momentum going with another impactful story.

Meanwhile, the tight-knit community was gripped by escalating violence and rampant drug abuse. Desperate, the mayor and local leaders had pleaded with the police department to address the worsening situation, but officials insisted they were "handling" it.

Nicole, driven by tenacity, found herself repeatedly warned to leave town and even threatened with jail. She had assured the police that her reporting would not cast them in a negative light, yet the deeper she dug, the more evidence surfaced of officers neglecting the law. Each new lead uncovered another instance of misconduct, and the list of corrupt officers seemed to grow longer by the day.

Into this charged environment stepped Nicole's long-absent biological father, James—an unexpectedly alluring distraction whose sudden appearance only added to the mounting drama. Nicole couldn't help but worry about the impact his presence would have on her and her family.

Sisters and
Secrets

Nicole requested a bottle of Tuscan red wine from the waiter before sitting down across from her older sister.

"It's been really wonderful having you here, Cynthia. I'm going to miss you when you leave. You really should have spoken to your lawyer before coming out; that way, you wouldn't have to leave so abruptly—just as I was getting used to having you around."

"We still need to sort out some child support details before wrapping everything up. The mediation shouldn't drag on long, since we both agreed on a fair amount for child support," Cynthia replied.

Cynthia was already halfway through her first glass, explaining how much colder it felt in her new apartment this March and how the heating bill was a small fortune.

Nicole nodded, but her eyes wandered over Cynthia's shoulder, drawn to the motion of a couple at a corner table. The man leaned in, whispering to the woman, his hand a soft weight on her arm. She laughed, her head tilting back, and the sound was like the clink of glass. He stood, pulling her up with an offered hand, and they glided toward the small dance floor, bodies aligning like pieces of a simple puzzle.

Nicole's body reacted to the scene, a sudden awareness like an unexpected blush. She wondered what it would feel like to be touched by a man, to be held by strong arms, to be pressed against a chest unlike her own. Her thoughts lingered on James, and she held herself in a daydream until she heard her name.

"Nicole?" Cynthia's voice was like a splash of cold water.

Nicole blinked, her cheeks warm, the room shifting back into focus. "Sorry," she said, trying to compose herself, though her heart was a startled bird. "I was miles away."

"Clearly." Cynthia gave her a half-amused, half-pitying look. "Were you listening to anything I said?"

"I was," Nicole insisted, smoothing the napkin in her lap as if it might iron out the awkwardness. "You were freezing to death in your apartment."

"Mmhmm," Cynthia murmured, her gaze sharp and searching, as if peeling back layers to find a hidden truth.

The waiter returned, pouring the wine into Nicole's glass. She took a big sip, the warmth of it curling through her chest. "Anyway, tell me about the kids. How are they holding up?"

"Alecia is off to her therapy session right now. We had to make sure that Frank would be okay before she agreed to go."

"And have they mentioned anything about his case?"

"Olivia's on it. She's taking on a self-defense case, which, of course, is riling up the families of the victims—if you want to call them that," Nicole said, pausing to signal the waiter for a glass of water.

"They're trying for a kid, by the way."

"Really? That's fantastic! But why am I the last one to hear about this?"

"Because you're so hard to get ahold of, dear. It took a stranger, of all people, to finally force you to slow down a bit."

Nicole took a sip of her wine. "I wouldn't say it was all his doing."

"I would say so. Let's be honest—one of the reasons I made the trip was because Dad insisted I meet Noah's biological father. And what better distraction than watching my little sister get all flustered around a man?"

"I wish I had kept that news to myself. And I wouldn't call it nervous; I'd say surprised—a massive, overwhelming surprise, that's all."

Cynthia chuckled. "So, are you saying this man doesn't have any effect on you? Because, according to Dad, you were visibly on edge when you spoke with him."

"Of course I am affected. We don't know anything about him or his background, so I'm justified in feeling uneasy until we figure it all out."

"Is that all?"

"That's it."

"Are you sure?"

"I'm sure."

"Fair enough. Completely understandable."

"Thank you."

"By the way, does he bother your vagina?"

"Cynthia!"

"You don't need to defend yourself, sis," Cynthia said. "It's perfectly fine if you find him attractive. I just want you to be happy and make decisions carefully. Lord knows our family hasn't always made the right choices. I'm sure Daddy is ecstatic."

"And you're not?" Nicole asked,.

Cynthia laughed softly. "I'm happy either way. Honestly, I'm not in a position to dish out advice right now. I've made some terrible choices that I have to deal with, and without my family, these past few months would have been much harder."

Nicole reached over and grabbed her hand in silent support.

"But truly, I have to come by more often. It's so good to reconnect with my baby sister again."

"Just like old times, right?"

"Minus the drama, jobs, kids, and, well, adulting," Cynthia grinned.

"And of course, Daddy's twenty-minute lectures about life's responsibilities and consequences."

"He means well. Both our parents come from an era where responsibility was instilled early. They passed that on to us, and it's shaped how we raise our kids—whether we'd like to admit it or not."

For most of Nicole's childhood and teenage years, she had followed her father's guidance without question. Sergeant Cornelius M. Winn had laid out meticulous family schedules—from meals to clothing choices and educational expectations. That structure worked perfectly until college, when she finally began to rebel against his authority.

"You don't need to tell me, Cynthia," Nicole said. "You don't think I'm aware of how my life choices upset everyone? In fact, that strict upbringing ultimately shaped my professional career, so in hindsight, it did help me."

"Are you admitting that Dad was right?" Cynthia protested.

"I never said that," Nicole replied dryly. "I think this wine is making your memory a bit foggy, don't you agree?"

"My memory's fine, thank you. I may be the eldest, but I still remember some of Dad's unreasonable parenting. When you finally decided to live your own life without his restrictions, I was right there cheering you on—even though a year-long silence between the two of you nearly drove us insane! But everything eventually worked out. Noah was born, your maternal instincts took over, and you rejoined the family circle. Your relationship with Dad has become stronger than ever."

Raising an eyebrow, Nicole teased, "Do you honestly believe that if Noah hadn't been born, Dad and I would have continued with the silent treatment?"

"I think you're both so alike that eventually you'd have reconciled anyway. Noah was simply the blessing that helped mend your bond."

Nicole smiled. "You always know the right thing to say. I had hoped you'd take your own advice when it came to your marriage. I was a bit disappointed when you called to say that you and Anthony were separating."

"Divorcing," Cynthia corrected sharply, reigniting their old debate about how to define her marriage. Nicole wasn't ready to use that word—Anthony had been part of the family since she was sixteen. In her eyes, he was more like a brother, and Cynthia's insistence on calling it a divorce felt like a definitive farewell that Nicole just couldn't accept. They both knew better than to argue further, so the topic quickly shifted.

Nicole called over the waitress and admitted, "All right, Cynthia, yes—I am attracted to James."

Cynthia placed a manicured finger to her ear and said, "Could you say that again? My hearing isn't what it used to be."

"Damn," Nicole laughed. "Just keep this from Dad as long as possible, okay? I need another bottle of wine."

"I can't drive while intoxicated, Nicole. You know Anthony's lawyers are just waiting for a slip-up."

"You'll be fine," Nicole reassured, pouring both their glasses halfway.

"That's what you said last time at La Rosetta, and you had to call Olivia to help you get me into the car in the middle of the afternoon while Anthony was campaigning in the area."

"You were a composed drunk, sis—thank you—and you actually managed to keep your dignity this time," Nicole replied playfully.

Cynthia's laughter drew a few curious looks from nearby tables. "I really don't know what I'd have done without you and Olivia. Those were some dark days for me and the kids, and my only solace was the long conversations with my sisters."

"I'm glad we could be here together."

"So, what's the plan from here? Have you thought about scaling back on the investigation?"

Nicole shook her head stubbornly. "I haven't given it much thought. No one else at the newsroom could approach this story with the same level of dedication and thoroughness that I do. I just can't envision handing it over to anyone else."

"It's dangerous, Nicole."

"Yes, I admit it's dangerous, and yes, Renée will have opinions on how it might affect our family—especially Noah. But if I don't see this investigation through completely, who will?"

"I agree. If not you, then who? But I believe this story, among other things, will change far more than you're expecting, dear sister. Blessings to you—I'm praying that God sees you through this."

"I'll drink to that," Nicole said.

They lingered at the restaurant, reluctant to say goodbye. Their hugs were a bit tighter, their farewells more heartfelt. Cynthia promised to call more frequently, while Nicole vowed to stay out of trouble, at least for the time being.

The walk to the parking garage felt unusually long. Nicole's small SUV was parked between a patrol car and an old Mustang. Despite trying to dismiss Cynthia's warning, a nagging feeling lingered—this new challenge might throw her family life off balance.

At her car, Nicole noticed several missed calls from Renée, but it was a message from James that immediately caught her attention. He wanted to talk at a specific time, and there was no avoiding that conversation anymore. As she got into her car, a chill ran down her spine despite the warm weather. This wasn't just a normal sensation; something was definitely off.

Nicole couldn't shake the image of James from her mind; his dark eyes seemed to follow her everywhere, even now as she sat at the breakfast table watching Noah doodle on the back of a cereal box. It had only been a few days since the party, since that mysterious man had entered their lives like a character from one of Noah's comic books, but already he felt woven into their routines.

Across the table, Noah was humming to himself, tongue peeking out of the corner of his mouth as he focused on drawing. Nicole smiled, ruffled his hair, and felt an inexplicable warmth spread through her. "Guess what?" she said, keeping her voice as casual as possible. "We might see James today."

Noah's eyes lit up. "Really? Is he bringing ice cream?"

"I think that can be arranged," she said, feeling a flutter of anticipation.

Later, as they walked to the park, Nicole carried a bundle of nervous energy, tinged with a thrill she couldn't deny. Her heart quickened at every movement, every shadow, half-expecting James to emerge before she even reached their meeting spot. Noah skipped a few steps ahead, kicking a stray leaf with superhero enthusiasm, and Nicole felt a pang of guilt for the way her thoughts centered around James. Was she being fair to Noah? To herself? To Renée? With every step, doubt mingled with excitement, creating a heady sense of uncertainty.

When they turned the corner of the park's entrance, she saw him. Leaning against a tree, hands in the pockets of his leather jacket, James's presence seemed to anchor the world around her. He looked up, and their eyes met. A slow, easy smile spread across his face, and Nicole felt herself melt.

"Hey, there," he called, a playful warmth in his voice.

Noah ran ahead, and James knelt to greet him, offering a fist bump that made Noah giggle with delight. Nicole approached him more slowly, savoring the sight of James and Noah together. There was a gentleness to their interaction, one she hadn't expected but found herself increasingly drawn to.

"Hey," she said, breathless despite herself.

James stood, brushing his hands on his jeans. "I brought something," he said, nodding toward a cooler at his feet.

Noah's eyes widened with glee, and James chuckled, lifting the lid to reveal an assortment of ice cream bars. "I thought you'd like these."

"Yes!" Noah exclaimed, reaching for a chocolate-covered treat.

Nicole laughed, the sound soft and surprised. "You're spoiling him," she said, a note of teasing in her voice.

"Is it working?" James asked, his smile tilting sideways with a hint of charm.

They found a spot under a sprawling oak tree, the late morning sun sprinkling the grass with patterns of light and shadow. Noah sat between them, happily munching on his ice cream, while James and Nicole exchanged glances that seemed to hold more than words.

Nicole leaned back on her hands, feeling the cool earth beneath her palms, grounding and calming her. Yet, the way James watched her, even when she looked away, sent her heart into a soft, erratic rhythm.

"How's business?" she asked, trying to steady herself with small talk.

"Busy," he said, shrugging a little, as if the word carried more weight than he let on. "But I like it that way."

Noah interrupted with a sticky hand on Nicole's knee. "Mom, can we go to the playground? Please?"

She hesitated, looking at James. "We can all go," she said, trying to read his expression.

James smiled, easy and reassuring. "I don't mind," he said, but the way he lingered on their faces made Nicole feel as if they were the only two people in the park.

As Noah raced ahead with singular focus, Nicole and James stayed back, walking in a companionable silence that buzzed with unspoken questions and tentative hopes. She watched Noah scrambling onto the play structure and turned to James, catching a flicker of something thoughtful in his eyes.

"He's really taken to you," Nicole said, trying to mask her vulnerability with a casual smile.

James kicked a small stone with the toe of his boot, watching it skip across the path. "He's a good kid," he said, his voice softer. "You're doing great with him."

A sudden rush of emotion caught her off guard. "I worry so much," she confessed, surprised at her own openness. "About what he needs and if I'm enough."

"You are," James said, and there was a firmness in his tone that made her believe him, even if only for a moment.

They reached the playground, where Noah was already swinging from a metal bar, pretending to be some caped crusader. James stopped beside her, his shoulder almost brushing hers, close enough that she could feel the warmth radiating from him.

"How about you?" Nicole asked, her voice tinged with curiosity. "Is this... I mean, do you think it's too much? Us, showing up in your life like this?"

James hesitated, and for a fleeting moment, he looked almost vulnerable. "Not at all," he said finally, glancing sideways at her. "I like having you around."

The sincerity in his words made her heart skip. She watched Noah slide down a pole, laughing and fearless, feeling as though she were sliding into something herself, something unknown and thrilling. Maybe it was the way James's presence seemed to envelop them, offering a sense of safety she hadn't realized she longed for.

They settled onto a bench, the playground alive with the sounds of children and birdsong. Noah dashed from one activity to the next, and Nicole relaxed into the rhythm of the afternoon, a new kind of lightness blooming in her chest. She turned, about to speak, when she noticed James's gaze shift briefly over her shoulder.

His face changed, just a flicker, before he returned his focus to her. "What is it?" she asked, acutely aware of every nuance in his expression.

"Thought I saw someone," he said, too casually, and she caught the edge of tension in his voice. He leaned forward, elbows on his knees, and the momentary shadow passed. "Guess I was wrong."

Nicole glanced back, scanning the park, but saw nothing except a jogger in the distance and a few parents chatting by the swings. She felt a chill that had nothing to do with the breeze.

Noah ran up to them, breathless. "Look, I can climb all the way to the top now!" He pointed triumphantly at the jungle gym, eyes wide with excitement.

"You're like Spider-Man," James said, rubbing Noah's head, but Nicole could hear the distraction beneath his playful tone.

"Watch me!" Noah called, already halfway back to the structure.

They watched him race off, and Nicole turned to James, searching his face. "Is there something I should know?"

He hesitated, the pause stretching between them. "No," he said, but the way he looked away made her wonder. "Everything's fine."

She wanted to believe him, wanted to trust this strange, fragile thing between them. She leaned back, trying to absorb the warmth of the sun and the sound of Noah's laughter. But the image of James's brief, wary glance lingered.

For the rest of the afternoon, they stayed in the park, the hours slipping by in a gentle, almost dreamlike blur. Nicole felt time stretch and bend around them, measured in shared smiles and the occasional brush of hands as they helped Noah with his shoes or caught him at the bottom of the slide. It was nearly dinner when they parted ways, their goodbyes lingering like the final notes of a favorite song.

But Nicole couldn't shake the feeling that they weren't alone, that someone—or something—was keeping pace with them. James's hesitation, the way his eyes had scanned the park, stayed with her, a shadow at the edge of all the warmth.

She walked home with Noah, trying to focus on his animated retelling of the day's adventures, but the chill of uncertainty trailed after her, dogged and persistent.

She set it aside as best she could, burying herself in the evening's rituals—dinner, bath, bedtime stories—each a comforting reminder that life wasn't so easily upended.

After tucking Noah in, she checked the locks twice, a precaution that felt both necessary and absurd. She sank into the couch; the house was quiet now, and she let herself replay the day's moments with James, trying to recapture the sense of closeness and calm. His face hovered in her thoughts, a mix of charm and uncertainty, and she found herself imagining what it would be like if he were there, fitting into their evening as seamlessly as he had that afternoon.

The hum of the refrigerator was the only sound in the dimly lit room, and Nicole felt the emptiness around her, stark and unsettling after the fullness of the day. She picked up her phone, stared at the screen, then set it down again. Was she really going to call him? It seemed too soon, too eager, but the impulse tugged at her, insistent and bold. Renée wasn't going to be home anytime soon.

Meanwhile, from across the street, a figure huddled in the shadows, watching through binoculars. The report had been clear: stay close but don't intervene. Guzman wanted a full account, and this watcher wouldn't disappoint. The woman, the boy, and the man who had made himself scarce for so long—each was a piece in a game until he had the whole puzzle. For now, patience and vigilance were the orders of the day.

The figure adjusted his position, peering through the lenses as Nicole reached for her phone again. The watcher saw her hold it, hesitate, and then press a button with resolve. The sensation of something about to happen pulsed in her, a beat she'd followed all day. She heard the first ring, her heart matching its tempo. Then another. On the third, just as she began to doubt, his voice came through, warm and unmistakable.

"Nicole?"

She released the breath she hadn't realized she was holding. "Hi. I—" She stopped, searching for an excuse that didn't sound as desperate as she felt. "I wanted to thank you for today."

His laugh was a low rumble, soothing and close despite the miles between them. "I should be thanking you. Best day I've had in a long time."

Nicole shifted, cradling the phone against her shoulder. "I wasn't sure if you'd be sick of us already."

"Not a chance," James said, and she could hear the sincerity in his voice, the smile she imagined playing across his lips.

Noah stirred in the other room, mumbling in his sleep, and Nicole felt a tenderness wash over her. "Noah had a great time," she said. "He wouldn't stop talking about how you helped him climb that tower."

"He's fearless," James replied, and there was something wistful in the way he said it.

"That's because he had a good role model today."

A pause stretched, gentle and full, before James spoke again, his tone shifting, more serious now. "Nicole, I—"

She held her breath, sensing something unspoken.

"I had a really great time," he said finally, and she could feel the weight of what he wasn't saying just beneath the surface.

"Me too." Her voice was soft, almost a whisper. "Maybe we can—"

"Tomorrow evening?" James interrupted, eager.

Nicole couldn't help but smile, the tension in her chest unraveling. "I'd like that."

"Then it's a date," he said, and she imagined the way his eyes must crinkle with his grin.

They lingered on the line, reluctant to disconnect, each holding on to the thread of connection.

When she finally hung up, Nicole sat in the quiet, a slow warmth spreading through her. The earlier chill dissipated, leaving only a sense of possibility. If only she didn't have to go to work tomorrow, she could spend the entire day with...James? She shook her head. She would have to give Renée the rundown of the day, but not right now. Right now, she just wanted to be in her own thoughts.

Outside, the watcher made a note, careful and precise. Guzman would be pleased with the progress. He'd keep vigil through the night, through the days to come, until his instructions changed. Nicole would never know the danger that threaded so closely around her, never suspect how tangled her life was becoming with the man and the history he carried with him.

But for tonight, there was just the feeling of hope, the promise of something new and bright. She tucked it away, close to her heart, and fell asleep with James's voice still in her ears.

In a house miles away, James paced the floor, wrestling with the urge to call her again. He was surprised at how much he wanted to, how easily Nicole and Noah had slipped past his defenses, and how much he already missed their presence. The evening had been tense, made worse by the sight of a familiar figure by the playground. But hearing Nicole's voice had dispelled some of the worry, and the possibility of seeing them again tomorrow filled him with a sense of urgency.

He stopped to peer out the window, scanning the street below. His instincts told him he was being watched, but he hadn't expected Guzman's men to find him so quickly. He glanced at the phone, considering his options, feeling the weight of decisions pressing in. Could he keep Nicole and Noah safe, or was he bringing danger too close?

The newsroom was alive. It pulsed with breaking news. The pursuit of truth was constant. Coffee and printers filled the air. Phones rang. Keyboards clattered.

In the midst of this controlled chaos, Nicole sat at her desk, her fingers dancing over the keyboard as she typed out her thoughts. Her desk was a testament to her dedication—stacks of papers, Post-it notes scribbled with reminders, and a mug of coffee that had long since gone cold. Her eyes, sharp and focused behind her glasses, scanned the documents spread out before her. The anonymous tip she had received was a ticking time bomb, and she could feel the weight of its potential reverberating through her chest.

As she gathered her notes and pushed her chair back, the wheels squeaked softly against the worn linoleum floor. She stood, her posture straight and confident, and made her way toward Albert Gray's office. The path was familiar, one she had walked countless times over the years, but today it felt different. The stakes were higher, the risks greater, and the potential impact of her story more profound than anything she had ever tackled.

Albert's office was a sanctuary of sorts, a quiet corner amidst the newsroom's frenzy. The door was open, as it always was, a silent invitation to his team. He sat behind his desk, leaning back in his chair, a stack of papers in one hand and a pen in the other. His gruff exterior belied the warmth and mentorship he offered to those who earned his respect. Nicole was one of them.

She knocked lightly on the doorframe, and Albert looked up, his eyes meeting hers with a mix of curiosity and concern. "Albert, I've got something big," she said, her voice steady but laced with an undercurrent of excitement.

He motioned for her to enter, his chair creaking as he leaned forward. "What's so important that an email wouldn't do, Nicole? I can tell by that look on your face that it's not your average story."

Nicole stepped into the office, the door closing softly behind her, shutting out the noise of the newsroom. She placed the documents on his desk, her hands steady despite the adrenaline coursing through her veins. "This file contains evidence that exposes the police force," she began, her voice low but firm. "We're talking bribery, corruption, extortion, and murder. It's extensive, involving high-ranking officials and connections to organized crime. We have a chance to blow the lid off this."

Albert's eyes narrowed as he scanned the papers, his brow furrowing deeper with each passing second. "This is explosive, Nicole," he murmured, his voice a low rumble. "If what you've got here is true, it could bring down some powerful people. But let's not forget the risks involved. We need to be careful."

Nicole nodded, her determination unwavering. "I understand the risks. I'm prepared to dig deeper and ensure that we have an airtight story. First, I'll try and get an interview with one of the officers at the police precinct. I don't expect either of them to snitch on their brothers in blue. But if I can just try to convince one of them to divulge some information, it would be helpful. We owe it to the public and to the honest cops who serve with integrity."

Albert leaned back in his chair, his gaze thoughtful as he contemplated their next move. "I don't like it, Nicole. Wait for my call before you run with it. Remember, this is going to put a target on your back. Stay vigilant and keep me updated every step of the way. This story has the potential to change the landscape of this city."

With a sense of purpose burning within her, Nicole rose from her chair, her mind already racing with the investigation ahead. She thanked Albert for his support, understanding that her journey was just beginning. As she returned to her desk, she felt a mix of anticipation and apprehension. The path she had chosen would be perilous, but her determination to uncover the truth burned brighter than ever. She picked up the phone and dialed the number for the police precinct, setting the appointment for one o'clock.

The newsroom buzzed around her, oblivious to the storm she was about to unleash.

The Pulse of the News

The police headquarters air was thick with the scent of stale coffee and the hum of voices echoing through the corridors. The walls were adorned with commendations and photographs of officers in action, a testament to the department's history and achievements. Nicole sat at a gray steel table in one of the interrogation rooms, her fingers tapping impatiently against the cold, unyielding surface.

Finally, the door creaked open, and Officer Carlos stepped inside. His presence filled the room, his broad shoulders and stern expression commanding attention. He carefully placed his jacket behind the chair and tucked his tie between his legs before taking a seat, his movements deliberate and calculated.

The room felt smaller with each fluorescent flicker. Officer Carlos's hands remained locked on the table as if shackled there, his eyes two slits of suspicion that pinned Nicole to her chair. She took a breath, steadying herself as she pushed the folder of documents his way. It caught the edge of his fingers, but he refused to flinch, his tight-lipped scowl showing nothing but contempt. "You're treading in dangerous territory, Ms. Winn," he growled, his pen tapping like a metronome.

Nicole's face held steady as she met his glare. "And you're in an awfully defensive position for a man with nothing to hide." Her fingers flipped the folder open, revealing the documents inside. Carlos's eyes darted to the pages, then back to her, the corners of his mouth twitching in disdain.

"You think this is going to scare me?" He leaned in, bringing the force of his presence to the narrow space between them.

"I think this is going to make you answer some questions," Nicole said, her voice a firm counterpoint to his bravado. She turned one of the papers toward him, her hand lingering on the edge as if offering a silent ultimatum.

Carlos didn't even glance at it. "What's your angle here?" His pen resumed its relentless rhythm against the metal table.

"My angle is the truth." Nicole sat back slightly, letting the weight of her words hang between them. "I have photos, financial records. I'm giving you a chance to explain your side."

He laughed, a short bark that echoed off the cinder block walls. "Explain my side? Is this an interview or an interrogation? Lady, you have no idea what you're stepping into." He paused, his smile sharp as glass. "Must be nice to hide behind a desk, thinking there are no consequences."

Nicole felt the crack in her armor where his words hit. "You mean like these?" she said, her fingers finding another paper in the stack. The print showed a man in uniform, his face unmistakable.

Carlos's expression faltered for just a moment before setting back into stone. "You call this evidence? That could be anyone."

"Really?" Nicole said, tilting her head. "You want to go on record with that statement? Because to me, it looks a lot like you."

His eyes flared, and for a moment, she saw the fight building in him. He leaned back, arms crossing his chest, affecting a posture of indifference that didn't quite mask the tightness in his jaw. "You know," he said slowly, "your family wouldn't appreciate what you're doing here."

A chill passed through Nicole, but she refused to let it show. "They appreciate honesty, Officer Carlos. They understand why I don't walk away from threats."

His mouth twisted, half smile, half sneer. "From where I'm sitting, all you've got is a stack of papers and a death wish."

Nicole's hand hovered over the image. "So, you're saying it's not you in this photo?"

"Damned right, it's not." Carlos's hands clenched tighter, his fingers white from the pressure.

She raised her eyes to meet his. "And this isn't your badge number? Or is your captain shaking hands with a known dealer?"

Carlos slammed a fist onto the table, the noise sharp and final. "You think you're clever, don't you?" he shouted, his composure unraveling with every word.

Nicole waited for the echo to fade. "I think I'm prepared," she replied. "You have no idea how many copies I have."

Silence stretched across the table as Carlos struggled to contain himself. His nostrils flared with each quick breath. The pen lay forgotten.

She leaned in, her tone quieter but no less assured. "All I want is the truth. Who are you protecting?"

His mouth opened, then closed. A tremor ran through his jaw, visible in the unforgiving light. "And how do you think this ends for you?" he said finally, the threat thinly veiled.

"With a story," Nicole replied. "And your captain out of a job. Maybe you too."

Carlos sat up, the muscles in his neck taut as wire. "You reporters think you can make up anything you want. You'll see how wrong you are."

Nicole shook her head, gathering the papers back into the folder. "We both know what's on those pages is real." She stood, smoothing her jacket. "Consider this a courtesy visit."

Carlos's eyes followed her every move, burning with an intensity that threatened to scorch. "You're putting your family at risk. This is the last time I'm telling you."

She hesitated, looking at him with something close to pity. "And this is the last time I'm asking you," she said.

He shifted his chair closer to the table, his hand almost touching Nicole's. It was a classic intimidation tactic; one she had seen many times before. She noted his paranoid glances toward the two-way mirror, his eyes darting nervously before settling back on her.

Nicole flipped through her notes, her eyes scanning the details of the reports she had gathered. "What is the department doing with rumors about some of your fellow policemen and their connection with drug dealers in the area?"

Carlos's expression darkened, his voice taking on a defensive edge. "They're rumors, that's all. If there was something going on to that magnitude, we would handle it, like we're trained to do."

Nicole pressed on, her voice firm and unyielding. "That's just it. There have been several incidents where the police were caught being the strong men for drug dealers, and citizens are frightened of what that could mean for their neighborhoods."

Carlos's jaw tightened, his voice sharp. "I don't recall any incidents, Mrs. Winn."

Nicole read aloud from their reports, her voice steady and clear. "Witnesses from those reports have come forward stating police involvement in a few drug busts looked a little suspicious when those that were arrested were quickly let go and allowed to leave the scene."

Carlos shifted uncomfortably in his seat, his expression growing more irritated by the moment. "I don't cover those arrests, plus they're outside my jurisdiction."

Nicole leaned forward; her eyes locked on his. "But they were in your former partner's area, Officer Blake."

At the mention of Blake, Carlos's posture stiffened, his eyes never leaving Nicole's face. A smirk settled around the corners of his mouth, a clear sign of his growing agitation.

"How's your nephew?" he asked, his voice laced with a mocking tone.

Nicole's expression remained composed, her voice steady. "My nephew is not a part of this interview, Officer Carlos."

Carlos leaned forward, his voice low and menacing. "He should be. As a matter of fact, have they charged him with homicide yet? I may investigate it. If I were his father, I would've finished the job; I can guarantee you that. He'll probably end up in the juvenile detention center, and I'm sure the court will appoint him a dumbass attorney who won't look after his case unless there's someone else you have in mind."

Nicole's grip tightened on her pen, her frustration mounting. "The questions I have for you are in relation to the upswing in drug activity in the county. How is the police department handling the increases in homicides and other crimes? And what measures have been taken to stop the narcotics?"

Carlos's eyes narrowed; his voice filled with contempt. "Our officers go out every day to keep these streets safe from people who want to use them for their own fun little playground. You should be thanking us instead of chastising us every chance you get."

Nicole's voice remained steady, her determination unwavering. "What about the officers that were recently indicted on drug charges?"

Carlos twisted in his seat, his discomfort palpable. "What about them?" he asked nonchalantly.

Nicole's voice was firm, her eyes unyielding. "They were indicted several days ago due to their involvement with dealers that are bringing methamphetamine and fentanyl onto the very same streets that they're supposed to protect."

Carlos's expression darkened, his voice taking on a cruel edge. "Are your boobs real?"

"Could you please answer the question, Officer Carlos?"

Carlos's smirk widened, his voice dripping with malice. "How about your wife? Are her boobs real?"

Nicole's eyes flashed with anger; her voice filled with indignation. "Irrelevant. My personal life has nothing to do with these questions, sir."

Carlos leaned forward, his voice low and menacing. "Tell me something—when you two have sex, who's the butch and who's the bitch?"

Nicole's patience snapped; her voice filled with frustration. "Our time is done, Officer Carlos," she said hurriedly, packing her things and heading for the door.

Carlos's laughter followed her; his voice was filled with mocking amusement. "Inquiring minds want to know."

Nicole's voice was sharp as she turned back to face him. "Thanks for your answers to my questions."

Carlos's smirk remained in place; his voice was filled with disdain. "Don't mention it."

Nicole's voice was filled with determination as she opened the door. "And I'll be sure to quote you accurately in the next article."

Carlos's voice was laced with sarcasm as he called after her. "When you get the picture, make sure you get my good side. It's the left side of screw you."

Nicole walked to the door, her steps firm and unfaltering. The camera panned over Carlos's taut form, capturing his rage and the slightest hint of doubt that furrowed his brow. Behind him, the fluorescent lights buzzed on, off, on.

Frustrated after a fruitless interview, Nicole slammed the SUV door and raced back to the office. She had invested months reporting this story and refused to be deterred by an arrogant source who stonewalled her questions. With no new leads, Nicole knew she needed to find another angle to pressure the police department. Compelled by her journalistic instincts, she hurried to update her editor, Albert, on the developments—or lack thereof. As Nicole pulled away, she noticed the police cruiser trailing behind her, a silent reminder of the ongoing struggle for truth and justice.

The next day, a burly man in a black shirt and jeans walked up and checked his license and weapon before passing through the security checkpoint. Nicole thought she recognized him as one of the officers she had seen at the police station recently.

Nicole and Rodney approached the desk, their footsteps echoing softly against the marble. The guard looked up, his expression shifting from stern to welcoming as he recognized them.

"Morning, Nicole and Rodney," he greeted, his voice a low rumble. "Busy day ahead?"

Nicole offered a polite smile, her mind already racing with the events of the morning.

"Always, Thomas. You know how it is."

Thomas nodded, his eyes flicking to the elevator as the doors slid open with a soft chime. "Heading up?" he asked, though it was more of a formality than a question.

"Yes, it seems like we have unwanted company awaiting us."

"And by unwanted company, you mean Captain Shaw. He's been here a couple of times, Mrs. Winn." He handed her the clipboard where the officer had signed his name. Was he here personally to snitch on her, or did he have another motive? She thanked him and met Rodney at the elevator door.

"Captain Shaw just went up," Nicole said, her voice laced with urgency.

"You think he's going to Albert's office?" Rodney said, balancing the coffee tray while hitting number seven. She could have been sarcastic at this moment, but Rodney was one of her best co-workers and confidants. Nicole began rehearsing what she was going to say to Albert when he found out where she'd gone earlier. He'd be pissed, but eventually he would understand her need to get some more information, even if it meant walking into the lion's den without a gun.

"Of course, he is," Nicole said, watching every number appear over top of the elevator door, as if by some miracle the door would magically open to the place she desperately needed to be right now, in front of her boss's door, listening to their conversation. The truth was she was nervous about what Shaw was telling her boss at this very moment. If only she had an inside view of his office. Reading lips wasn't that hard, right?

Nicole entered the newsroom, her hands gradually being filled with paperwork from co-workers eager to get documents into her hands. Struggling to balance the items, she nearly dropped the folder before finally slamming it onto Rodney's desk, causing her white blouse to flutter. Rodney's eyes immediately fixed on the exposed top of her breasts. "Lesbians have great tits."

"How many harassment charges do you have, Rodney?"

"Apparently not enough. You know I acknowledge beautiful women when I see them, and a great pair of tits is a great pair of tits."

"And what about Ashley?"

"We're still kickin' it. She knows that I'm the polyamorous, bisexual, non-committal type."

"And your other partners are okay with this?"

"Of course, they are. They know I sleep with women. I'm gay, but I'm not that gay. Get it?"

Three people chimed in. "No."

Rodney navigated the new box of casefiles like a practiced archaeologist, extracting fragments of story from the debris and brushing off layers of dust. He spread the documents across the battered desk, a sea of photographs and redacted memos that left Nicole dizzy with their implications. "Look at this line item," he said, stabbing at a page with his finger. "It connects the captain directly to drug shipments." Nicole felt the evidence click into place with a sickening certainty.

They leaned over the desk, shoulder to shoulder, scanning the overwhelming amount of information. "And here," Nicole said, pointing to a blurred image, "isn't that the same officer from last month's surveillance?"

Rodney adjusted his glasses, studying the photo. "Could be. The same figure pops up in the Baldwin Gardens set. Might even be Carlos again." His fingers tapped the paper thoughtfully, then reached for another document.

The room felt like it was closing in, stacks of papers towering around them, turning the office into a labyrinth of unsorted clues. "If we're right," Nicole said, picking up the redacted memo, "then this is much bigger than one precinct." Maybe even the whole district."

Rodney pushed his glasses up and arranged another row of photos. "Which means the captain could have friends in high places," he said. His voice held both awe and the exhaustion of someone who'd been down this road too many times.

"Do you think we have enough for a story?" Nicole's pen scratched across her journal, the sound harsh and insistent in the close quarters.

"For a whole series," Rodney said, stacking photos of shadowy figures exchanging envelopes. His movements were steady, methodical, and precise, the perfect counterpoint to Nicole's more frantic notetaking.

She paused, overwhelmed by the sheer volume of it all. "How deep do you think this goes?" Her words were barely above a whisper.

Rodney studied her for a moment before answering. "All the way to the top. Maybe further." He picked up a sheet, crossing the room to dig for more in an unmarked box. "Especially if this came from Carlos."

Nicole closed her eyes briefly, letting the enormity of their task settle. Rodney noticed, pausing to offer a rare moment of reassurance. "We'll get it, Nicole. We always do."

The sound of the clock ticking somewhere under the piles spurred them back into motion. Nicole flipped through more photos, her eyes scanning for any missed detail. "It's the same players every time," she said. "This is huge, Rodney."

He joined her again, both of them poring over the prints. "And consistent," he added. "Whoever shot these knew exactly what they were doing."

"Who else has this?" Nicole's eyes were intense, catching Rodney's as they both considered the risks.

"If anyone else does, they're dead or hiding," Rodney replied. The gravity of his statement hung between them like a third presence.

Nicole didn't flinch. She moved with renewed urgency, planning out loud. "First we track down everyone in these photos, get statements, and confirm locations. We work around the clock if we have to."

Rodney glanced at the clock again, the pressure of their deadline visible on his face. "You don't think Carlos will tip them off?"

"Not if he thinks I'm scared," Nicole said, a fierce edge to her voice. "He doesn't know what we're holding yet."

Rodney frowned, unconvinced but loyal. "You know they'll come after you."

"They already are," she replied, undeterred. "Which is why we move fast."

Rodney fell silent, his hands working the documents into logical piles. He trusted her judgment, but the stakes had never been this high. He handed Nicole another photo, his eyes reflecting the shared risk they were taking. "Make sure you get home tonight."

Nicole finished a last note in her journal, a determined glint in her eyes. "Once we nail these bastards," she said, the words a promise. She looked at Rodney, their mutual resolve clear.

"We've got to get this out," Rodney said, watching her gather the papers. Their situation was desperate, but there was no one he'd rather be in it with.

"Nicole, I need to see you in my office now."

Albert bellowed his command from across the newsroom, while she walked past wide-eyed, curious faces and closed his door.

"I should've spoken with you a little more about your involvement in this story. You may need to keep a low profile due to your nephew standing trial soon. The police may use your nephew's story to try and knock you off your game."

"Too late. They know Frank is my nephew. Olivia is taking the case. Is there any news on our source? I tried calling the phone number in the files earlier, but their phone went straight to voicemail."

"I'll send one of our other reporters to try and get into contact with them. Hopefully we can get some more details on what's been happening."

"Thanks, Albert."

"Don't mention it. I don't want them to get wind of your connection to our source to use it against the piece we're about to reveal along with who's responsible for the narcotics in the county."

"What did the chief say to you?"

"Just that he doesn't appreciate our journalists harassing his hard-working officers. And if we continue, he'll press charges against us. He's an arrogant son of a bitch, but he's smart. I thought I said wait for my call. I should've known you wouldn't listen.

He took off his glasses and pinched the bridge of his nose.

"We need to play this as close to the letter as possible, which means getting every possible lead you can and beating them with solid facts. They'll be mad enough to kill. But at least we'll have solid evidence."

"Where is he?"

"He left about ten minutes ago. Got into a nice sixty-seven Shelby Mustang. Do you know how much those cars cost? Never knew a cop could afford that kind of car on their salary. We watched him on the security camera."

"Should I be worried about this, Albert? This isn't like the other stories we've handled."

"If we need to take drastic measures to ensure your safety, then we will. But I doubt that we'll need to go that far. Besides, no editor hired here has ever gone to that extreme for their journalist."

"Hopefully I won't be the first one."

Nicole thought of that last statement as she made her way back to her desk. She didn't know if Albert would be willing to go that extra mile for her and her family, and that bothered her. No other journalist was willing to take this story because not only was it dangerous, but it involved a lot of important people in higher positions. She was willing to take the risk. Another Pulitzer would look great for her career, but was it worth her life?

"What did old Albert say?"

"He thinks I should keep a low profile. Between my nephew's case and this one, he's worried that it could be more trouble for me than it's worth."

"He does have a point. Are you going to go through with it?"

"The community needs to know what the police are up to. Do we just let this go and pretend the drugs and corruption of law enforcement don't exist? How do we look our friends and neighbors in the face knowing this is happening and doing absolutely nothing about it?"

"I get it. And it's what you want to do, Sojourner Truth. Just know I've got your back with whatever decision you decide to make.

"Good to know."

"One more thing."

Nicole looked at him.

"This is unlike any story you've ever done before, and maybe I'm just a little nervous when I say this."

"Spit it out."

"I'd like to live through this if you don't mind."

He grabbed his chair to sit directly in front of her.

"All jokes aside, this is some serious stuff. People have come up missing, cops are getting off with not so much as a slap on the wrist, and the district attorney isn't doing a damn thing."

"I know, it's hard for me to stomach looking at him right now."

"Just promise me that we'll survive this. I'm way too young to die. I have a lot more life in these loins, if you know what I mean."

They moved together toward the door, leaving the office an organized chaos behind them, the urgency palpable in their every step.

The bureau spat them out into the Baltimore night. Rain and neon mingled to paint the streets an insidious shade of pink, glistening underfoot as Nicole and Rodney made their way into the alley. A plain black sedan lurked near the streetlamp like a predator in wait, its engine a low purr that sent adrenaline pumping through Nicole's veins.

Rodney hesitated, catching her arm as she fished for her phone. The screen blinked with an anonymous message: "Back off, or else." She showed it to him without a word, the terse warning punctuating the heavy air between them.

"Think it's Carlos?" Rodney asked, eyes fixed on the car's tinted windows. The lamp overhead flickered ominously, casting rhythmic shadows that heightened the sense of exposure.

"Or someone worse,"

Nicole said, straightening her jacket with defiance. "Let's get moving."

They shared a quick, understanding look and stepped into the alley, the black sedan a persistent shadow behind them. Their footsteps echoed against the brick walls, mingling with the steady hum of the car and the distant cry of a siren. Rain dripped from fire escapes and gutters, a slick, relentless patter that only added to the tension.

"They're definitely following us," Rodney said, his voice barely audible over their hurried footfalls.

Nicole nodded, gripping the folder tightly under her arm. "Let's cut through here," she said, pulling him into a narrower side street. The sedan crept behind them with a menacing patience.

Rodney glanced over his shoulder, the dark shape of the vehicle an ever-present threat. "Any chance it's a coincidence?" he asked, though they both knew the answer.

Their pace quickened as they emerged from the alley onto another rain-slicked street. Nicole's heart pounded in time with the adrenaline that coursed through her. "We have to lose them," she said, the words a fierce whisper.

They crossed through another alley, the car's tires hissing on the wet pavement as it kept a steady pursuit. Nicole and Rodney moved with urgent strides, breath misting in the cool night air. The city around them felt alive with threat, every corner and shadow a potential danger.

"Let's split up," Nicole said, making a split-second decision. "Meet back at the office if we shake them."

Rodney hesitated, the thought of leaving her visibly paining him. "Are you sure?"

"They won't risk being seen chasing both of us. Go!" Nicole's eyes flashed with determination, her conviction as unwavering as ever.

Rodney gave a reluctant nod and veered into another side street. The sedan followed Nicole, its headlights cutting through the dark and casting long, sinister shadows ahead of her.

She ran, her footsteps a rapid staccato on the glistening asphalt. Nicole darted through alleys and side streets, zigzagging through the urban maze. Her chest burned with exertion and fear, but she refused to slow down.

The car was relentless, tailing her with cold precision. Nicole could feel the danger nipping at her heels, a constant, oppressive presence that refused to relent.

Finally, she turned a sharp corner and pressed herself against the wet brick of a building, catching her breath. She peered around the edge, watching as the sedan's taillights flickered and disappeared into the Baltimore night.

Her heart thundered in her chest as she clutched the folder tighter, the evidence now more crucial—and more perilous—than ever. Nicole took a moment to collect herself, then moved quickly down the street, every sense on high alert for the threat she knew was far from gone.

She knew what she was doing.

Her dark hair tumbled over his thighs, cascading down to the floor as her lips glided over him. He was unable to grasp the back of her hair as he had previously; instead, she took all of him in her mouth, suppressing the reflex to gag and taking great pleasure in witnessing his unraveling. She quickened her pace, deep throating with each stroke, his groans growing more intense with every moment. He could feel the heat building between his legs, and with each downward motion she made, he was drawn further into a blissful void.

She suckled and suckled with a rhythmic swirl, encouraging him to build towards his peak. Then, she teased the tip of his sex before trailing her tongue down the length to the sensitive area beneath his balls. That was the tipping point. He released completely into her mouth, and with a final shudder, he pushed her away. Massaging his temples slowly, he leaned his head back against the chair's support. She wiped the remnants of his orgasm away with an off-white handkerchief. "Será todo por esta noche, señor Guzmán?" Is that all for this evening, Señor Guzman?

"Si, gracias, Emilia. Tell your husband, Marcos, I will see him this Sunday Mass."

She reached up to redo her ponytail and adjust the pins in her hair before exiting the room.

Guzman touched the intercom button for his driver. "Call the airport; we're leaving in an hour.

Time was running out. Guzman was going to have to leave New York with everyone thinking he foiled another attempt at killing her again. They'd begin to call him soft, untrustworthy, a failure, he guesses, and although they didn't realize the lengths he went to kill this woman, the word on the street would be the same as it had been the day he began his plans. Guzman simply didn't have any other choice. He'd already sent for his best assassin to meet him in West Virginia, but the man seemed to be busy with other assignments and hadn't bothered to respond. He was getting agitated by the minute. There simply wasn't enough time to placate the other bosses and keep the Feds out of his affairs. His businesses were at stake, and Jesús was the only one who would—or, more specifically, was hired—to do the job.

If the other bosses believed he couldn't handle one simple contract to kill a little flea of a woman, so be it. There was one last detail he needed taken care of. He'd been on to him since Nicole Winn picked back up her investigation of his business in the Old Line State.

Another few minutes passed before the door of the hotel room swung open once more. Rodriguez' sour expression, along with a neatly compiled envelope, stepped into the room. He was dressed in his usual expensive suit with emblem-stamped loafers; however, the collar was soiled as if he'd been sweating profusely before he got there. He attempted to look somewhat put-together, combing his hair back from his forehead in a futile effort at grooming as he placed the folder in front of Guzman.

"You're not going to like this, Guzman, Williams is alive and living in Maryland," he announced. "He lives about twenty minutes from Mrs. Winn and clearly doesn't want to be seen," he added. "I should've killed him myself years ago, sir. Your driver said you're leaving in an hour; I can come with you to see that he's finally taken care of."

Rodriguez followed Guzman to the elevator, wiping the sweat from his brow. He oversaw the man that supposedly killed Williams ten years ago. The stone-cold look Guzman gave him made him nervous while he eagerly waited for his response to his offer.

The slap that came next took him by surprise, but the several punches that followed set Rodriguez to the ground so fast he didn't have time to react. By the time the elevator reached the lobby floor, Rodriguez's face and collar were covered in blood. Guzman straightened the tail end of his suit and adjusted his tie. He wiped blood from his newly purchased rings and placed the handkerchief in Rodriguez' pocket, turned towards the opening elevator door, and said, "You think I didn't know?"

The men lounging against the wall stood at attention when they saw Guzman's face, hurriedly assisted him outside, and got into the second SUV to follow him to the airport. Guzman, however, paid no attention to the small spectacle he created as he ordered his driver to call the pilot to prepare the plane for takeoff. It would take almost an hour to get to the airport, but he wasn't deterred by the traffic. This time he would see to it that the job was done. He picked up the ringing cell phone, taking a moment to remove his gloves and set them on the empty seat beside him before finally turning his attention to the man hired to oversee the assassin. His voice was calm with a sinister quietness as he asked, "Have you gotten in touch with the man yet? There cannot be any more mistakes, Carlos, or I swear there will be hell to pay when I see you."

"I'm at the hotel now," Carlos said. He was trying to sound cool, but he could feel the shakiness in his voice. He tried to take deep breaths, which seemed to work a little. "I had to see him for myself; the man doesn't like answering phone calls."

Guzman ended the call. The hired gun was one of the best in the nation, if not the Western Hemisphere. He didn't miss his targets. And neither did Guzman. Some would ask why he waited this long to kill one person. Her pregnancy took her out of commission for nine months, with an additional year of breastfeeding.

Nothing he ever did was simple, and he waited for the opportune time to tell her he was the father. Some would call that insanity. He would state it simply as a plan that came to fruition. When he learned, however, that James was the father, he had to rewrite his plans, as they now included another mark. And James clearly was, if not even more difficult to kill than the woman was. James quickly took out five of the men Guzman sent immediately to kill him after verifying he was the father. And every time after that, another body would show up, belonging to Guzman's cartel, alerting police that something was afoot. Guzman couldn't stand to lose any more men or bring any more attention to himself. He decided to wait it out, to plan before his next move. The plane sat at the tarmac ready for takeoff when the four SUVs pulled up. The stewardess sensed something was clearly wrong, as all ten men rushed past her without a greeting to get on. She quickly regained her composure and took her seat opposite the cockpit. Their destination would take an hour and thirty minutes, which meant he could rest before speaking to his associate. Guzman had only one thought before closing his eyes: that Nicole Winn would finally be dead and James Williams would quickly follow the same fate.

West Virginia

The man gazed at his partially shaved reflection in the bathroom mirror, then rinsed the loose hairs from his razor in the sink. His cold, blue eyes studied the progress as he meticulously cleaned the area, ensuring no trace of his grooming remained. Satisfied the overgrown beard was sufficiently trimmed, he glanced at the phone beside him as it lit up, indicating a new text—the latest in a steady stream over the past couple weeks. With a sigh, he pressed 'message,' hoping this time it wasn't from the cop but rather the boss overseeing his contract.

Have you acquired the target?

Yes.

ETA.

He studied the black lettering of his response and pressed the reply button. The surveillance team had provided a detailed account of what he could expect. His target lived in a two-story house with minimal security, aside from a few cameras. Her only potential threat was her retired veteran father, who didn't seem particularly alarming.

There were no indications that she had contacted James Williams, but Guzman's frantic calls told him what he needed to know. He'd been on the run for years, so he was always a step ahead and easily avoided capture. Instinct for survival meant that Nicole Winn would also be on the move soon, and his window of opportunity was closing. He had dealt with more complex contracts, and there was little doubt in his mind this one would end any differently than other easy marks.

Tomorrow.

He packed the gun back into its case and picked up the phone before stepping over the dog-eared map of Maryland on the floor. The woman was incredibly resourceful; she escaped every attempt to kill her, even while pregnant. Guzman emptied out half his roster trying to catch her off guard until it became too costly to pursue her. Months turned into years as his target continued her investigations without fear of retaliation. She'd grown confident in her ability to dodge him at every turn, but that confidence would soon end.

On Saturday, her life would be snuffed out, and he would move on to the next target. He gazed out the hotel window in Harpers Ferry, West Virginia, overlooking the Appalachian Mountains, but forced himself to stay focused. He had a job to do.

Sitting with his arm rested against the chair, he poured another cup of coffee and took a long sip before turning his attention to the gun case on the table. He unsnapped both buckles, revealing the black silencer pistol nestled in its dark grey cushioned mold. Guzman had gifted him the suppressor as a commemoration of his twenty-fifth kill a few weeks prior. The other hired guns had voiced their preference for the 9mm's

15-round capacity, but he had simply remarked, "I only need one shot." They had quickly left, heads down, to continue their discussion of favoritism outside the massive mansion.

His cell phone rang with a familiar number. He accepted the call but remained silent. This cop was starting to irritate him.

"I don't suppose you could answer my phone calls since this is an emergency."

"I was busy."

"Oh yeah, doing what?"

"Watching the sunrise."

"Christ, a fucking poet with a gun."

"What do you want, Carlos?"

"Could you not say my name over an open airway?"

"You called a burner phone."

"I've seen the Fed put a mic in a stick of gum. You think a burner phone will stop them?"

"Two minutes."

"Your response to my earlier text was vague."

"I don't work for you, Carlos."

"Look, if this bitch gets the word out about what we've been doing, our department is finished. I'm talking pensions, incomes, kids' tuition—you name it. Our asses are on the line here."

"And your point?"

"Just take care of her soon. This is starting to bug you-know-who, and he doesn't take kindly to unfinished business."

"Is that a threat?"

"Just get it done."

He looked at the silencer and took a deep breath. One round, and his bank account would reflect the fifty thousand he was promised. Over the lush green forest, blooming wildflowers, and fall foliage, he heard the tumbling waters of the Potomac and watched from his balcony as the locals went about their day carefree, without worry. Unbeknownst to them, they were in the presence of a notorious hitman.

Fiery Embrace

Nicole's lips moved feverishly over Renée's glistening clitoris, each caress igniting a relentless fire until Renée could no longer contain the overwhelming surge of pleasure. In a desperate embrace, Renée's thighs locked around Nicole's face as she ground against her, riding out tumultuous waves of orgasm that reverberated through every nerve. She called James earlier to cancel their evening meet-up, and what was meant to be a serene evening alone—with Noah off visiting his grandparents—had been tainted by the day's earlier explosive events. Nicole's mind churned with unsettling thoughts as she waited for the storm of Renée's breaths to subside before she slipped off the bed's edge.

"Your turn," Renée murmured, her tone heavy with both desire and quiet unrest.

Nicole briskly wiped away the lingering traces of saliva, a subtle gesture that did not escape Renée's notice, though she chose to let it slide. Something was off with

Nicole tonight. "No, it's just you tonight. I have too much boiling inside my head," she confessed, her voice taut with urgency.

Renée's retort was laced with both longing and exasperation. "It's been weeks since we had a moment just for us, and now you're drowning in your own thoughts?"

"Yes, I'm covering a major story. There are drug dealers and police corruption tied to the mayor that need investigating." *And I'm developing feelings for a man I barely know.* Nicole's tension was evident.

Renée dismissed it: "Yes, there are bigger issues—greed and police brutality—plaguing the city. I'm sure there's someone at your office besides you who can handle the investigation." As she spoke, her kisses trailed along Nicole's neck, and her nipples grazed Nicole's back, a silent invitation to more intimacy. But tonight wasn't the time.

Nicole stood up, determined to have a direct conversation. Physical passion wouldn't mend the turmoil inside her.

"So, what is really bothering you? What else is on your mind?" Renée asked gently.

Nicole ran a frustrated hand through her hair. Unable to reveal her true feelings, she changed the subject. "This new story has me on edge, and I feel like I can't get a grasp on it. Like, there's something missing that I'm not getting."

Renée moved behind her, wrapping her arms around Nicole and planting a tender kiss on the nape of her neck, her hands soothingly rubbing Nicole's shoulders as she turned her around slowly. "Don't let yourself become overwhelmed with this story. You worry too much. Now, come back to bed."

"I need to go downstairs for a bit. I'll be back soon." Nicole grabbed her pajama bottoms from the chair and gathered her laptop from the lounge. For the first time ever, she left Renée standing alone and exposed.

In the living room, Nicole settled quietly, her notes from the previous day scribbled on a black-and-white pad labeled "truth and accuracy." She switched on her favorite ocean sounds, closed her eyes, and felt the heavy weight of the day begin to lift as the sound of crashing waves filled the room. Longing to feel the ocean wind on her face, she resigned herself to wait until later in the year. She uncorked a red wine bottle, poured a glass, and set it on the countertop.

Outside, the sun had just set, leaving a vibrant blend of orange and blue across the sky. Wind chimes danced in the rhythm of the last breeze before nightfall.

Nicole glanced halfheartedly at a box of documented reports tucked in the corner beside the couch. Albert had sent them over a pile of allegations detailing law enforcement misconduct. Yet she couldn't shake the feeling that something vital was missing—a final Hail Mary. She recalled an interview with a nervous officer whose anxious eyes kept darting to the door as if expecting intruders. Abruptly, he had ended the interview with a well-timed diversion, clearly hiding something.

Trailing him might yield answers, but it meant acquiring an inconspicuous car and a police radio—a risky endeavor. If she could muster the courage to follow him without being noticed, perhaps she could uncover the secrets the officer—and the entire department—were concealing. Her instincts screamed that something was amiss, and she had learned long ago to trust those feelings.

Just as she decided to wrap up her research for the night, her phone rang.

"Hello?" she answered.

A tense voice crackled through, "I need to see you immediately. There are people following me. I think they know I'm working with you, and it's freaking me out."

"Mr. Graham, slow down. Who's following you?" Nicole asked.

"The police. You promised my name and whereabouts would remain safe."

"I did. No one knows you're our informant."

"Then someone must have leaked my information, and now I've got these shadows on my trail. Fix this, Winn, fix it now!"

The line went dead, leaving only a dial tone. Who could be the one to betray such sensitive, life-altering information to the police? And more urgently, who had accessed her private notes on her home computer? Curling up on the couch, her body stiffened with resolve. She needed to find the source of the leak, and fast.

In the morning, Nicole awoke to the insistent hum of suburban life filtering through the curtains. The wineglass sat untouched, a dried crimson ring staining the counter like a forgotten promise. She checked her phone, hoping for some contact from Graham or any hint of his safety. Nothing.

Her breath caught as she remembered leaving Renée alone upstairs. There had been no quiet midnight return to bed, no whispers in the dark to smooth over the jagged edges of their night. Guilt mixed with defiance, she texted Albert to secure a private meeting space for an off-the-record catch-up with Graham.

Downstairs, she found Renée cheerfully setting out two steaming mugs of coffee and a plate of crumbs where toast had once been. "Busy night?" Renée asked without looking up, her voice tinged with something unreadable—accusation or concern or both.

Nicole blinked, trying to shrug off her fatigue. "I lost track of time."

"Hard at work, I see," Renée said, gesturing to the laptop. Her voice carried a hint of reproach mixed with understanding.

"It's complicated," Nicole admitted, rubbing her eyes.

"You think everything is complicated."

"That's because it is." Nicole sighed, shutting the laptop and setting it aside. The conversation with Mr. Graham had rattled her more than she wanted to admit, and she found herself staring at Renee, wishing she could articulate her fears better.

Renée's eyes softened as they locked onto Nicole's. "You're spread too thin, honey. Something is going to give."

"And what if it already has?" Nicole wondered aloud, frustrated by her own vulnerability. She took a sip of coffee, letting it scald her tongue in an effort to wake up.

"Then I'll be here to catch you." Renée reached across the table and touched Nicole's hand, a gesture of reassurance that felt both familiar and new after the night's tension.

They sat in silence for a moment, suspended between the possibility of understanding and the inevitability of more words. Finally, Nicole let out a deep breath. "I should check on Noah."

"He's still at his grandparents' until Sunday," Renée reminded her with a knowing smile. "And he's fine."

Nicole hesitated, then stood abruptly. "I just need to clear my head."

"Wait," Renée insisted, rising with Nicole. "You can't keep running from everything, especially me."

"I'm not running," Nicole replied, but the words felt hollow even to her own ears. She grabbed her coat from the hook by the door, and just like that, she was gone.

Cold air stung her cheeks as she hurried through their neighborhood. Streetlights flickered on, one by one, casting long shadows that stretched ahead of her like accusatory fingers. A few houses down, families laughed over dinner; farther up the street, a father tossed a football with his son. Nicole walked faster.

She ducked into the cafe where they were regulars and ordered a coffee she didn't really want. The barista eyed her curiously as he handed it over, but she was too distracted to care. She sank into a booth at the back, staring blankly out the window while her mind spiraled. The café buzzed around her with the sounds of steaming milk and quiet conversations. A couple at the next table bickered quietly over a crossword puzzle, the woman tapping her pen impatiently while the man squinted at the paper. Nicole envied them briefly, their simple companionship unmarred by deeper complications.

Renée was right about one thing: something had already given way. The arrival of James had split the delicate balance of their life apart, exposing fault lines she never knew existed. She sipped her coffee, barely tasting it, as she thought of Noah—a ten-year-old boy with questions she couldn't answer, a presence suddenly made solid and terrifying by his biological father's appearance.

Her phone vibrated on the table, rattling against the wood. She snatched it up, hoping for news from Graham or Albert. Instead, a message from Renée lit up the screen: "Come home when you're ready. I love you."

The words twisted in her chest painfully before loosening into something like relief. She turned off her phone and began to give.

"Mind if I sit?" A familiar voice jolted her back to the present. James stood over her, a sheepish grin on his face.

Nicole's heart skipped, then settled into a rapid patter. "How did you find me?" she blurted, more sharply than she intended.

He slid into the booth, hands held up in surrender. "I went by your house. Renée said you might be here."

The mention of Renée stung, and Nicole fought the urge to get up and leave.

Her eyes lingered on James, watching the way he scanned the room with a subtle, practiced sweep. It was as if he were always two steps ahead, always ready to protect.

She tried to lighten the air between them. "So, how do we do this?" she asked, more seriously than she intended.

"Do what?" James replied, though she could tell he knew exactly what she meant.

"Us," she said, the word hanging between them with a mix of hope and uncertainty. "You and me. And Noah...Renée."

James leaned back, letting the question sink in. "Carefully," he said, his smile teasing but his voice steady.

"That sounds... ominous," Nicole said, but the tension in her shoulders eased a bit. She traced a finger along the edge of the table, watching his expression.

"Does it scare you?" he asked, and she heard the real question beneath the lightness.

She met his gaze, her own steady. "Not yet."

A flicker of relief passed over his face, and he reached across the table, his hand settling over hers. His touch was gentle but certain, and Nicole felt the flutter of reassurance in her chest.

"We'll figure it out," he said, and she believed him, if only because she wanted to so much.

A waitress appeared, and they ordered coffee and pie, the simple act another thread in the tapestry they were weaving. James's hand stayed over hers, anchoring them together as the night spilled out in small talk and shared laughter. The unease of the morning receded, though Nicole sensed it was never too far from the edges, waiting for its chance to reemerge.

After the pie was gone and the coffee cups emptied, they lingered in the booth, reluctant to let the day end. Nicole studied the lines of James's face, the way his eyes softened when they rested on her, and she felt a warmth that pushed back against the shadow of his earlier apprehension. She wanted to reach across the table again, to hold on to him, but instead she glanced at her watch, breaking the spell.

"I should get back," she said, though leaving was the last thing she wanted.

James nodded, though she could see a touch of reluctance in his eyes. "I'll walk you," he said, sliding out of the booth beside her.

Outside, the air was sharp and bracing, and Nicole shivered as James draped an arm around her shoulders. They walked close, her head brushing against his jacket, an easy intimacy that felt like a beginning, like the first page of a book they were writing together.

As they neared her house, Nicole felt the sense of intrusion return, a watchful presence that made her skin prickle. She looked at James, who seemed to sense it, too. His grip tightened just a fraction, and they moved a little quicker, steps in sync.

"Here we are," she said, trying for lightness as they reached her door.

James hesitated, his eyes scanning the street, the windows, and the shadows pooling in corners. Then he kissed her near the corners of her mouth, the kind of kiss that promised more than words, that held the weight of everything both said and unsaid between them.

"Tomorrow?" he asked, his forehead resting against hers.

She nodded, feeling the loss of him already, knowing she'd count the hours. "Tomorrow."

Nicole watched him go, his figure receding into the darkness with a quiet confidence that both comforted and unsettled her.

Turning back, she saw Renée through the window, calmly folding laundry. The sight grounded her, reminded her of the life they had built, the life she couldn't imagine losing. She hesitated on the porch, her hand hovering over the doorknob. For a moment, she considered turning back, but exhaustion and the promise of Renée's steady presence pulled her inside.

Renée looked up as the door clicked shut. "I was starting to think you'd skipped town," she teased, though her eyes searched Nicole's face anxiously.

Nicole sank into a chair, the exhaustion of the day draping over her like a heavy blanket. She appreciated having Renée around for a welcome distraction, but it also left her feeling... vulnerable and exposed. She stared at the floor, unsure where to begin.

"Something happen?" Renée prodded gently, setting down the laundry and giving Nicole her full attention.

Nicole hesitated; a thousand words tangled on her tongue. "I saw James," she admitted finally, watching Renée's reaction carefully.

Renée went still, a crease forming between her brows. "And?"

"And he said he wants to be part of Noah's life," Nicole replied, her voice strained. "He said he's not here to make things harder."

"Do you believe him?" There was no accusation in Renée's question, just an openness that made Nicole want to lay everything bare.

"I don't know what to believe right now," Nicole confessed, leaning into the uncertainty of it all. "But he's not going away."

Renée came over and knelt beside her, taking Nicole's hands in hers. "Then we'll figure it out together," she said with quiet conviction.

She reached for her laptop instinctively, opening it with the intention of diving back into work as an escape from her tangled emotions. The inbox blinked with unread messages, but one from Albert caught her eye immediately: "FOUND A SAFE PLACE FOR YOU-KNOW-WHO. CALL ME."

With renewed energy she grabbed her phone and dialed.

Albert picked up before it had a chance to ring twice. "Winn? I thought you were ghosting me."

"Funny," she replied, relieved by the familiarity of his sarcasm. "You found a spot for Graham?"

"Yeah, but you better get your ass down here fast. He's paranoid as hell and keeps saying he's going to bail any second."

"Is he safe?" Nicole asked, remembering his frantic call and the way he'd ended it.

"For now," Albert said. "But I wouldn't bet on him sticking around for long."

Nicole weighed her options quickly—Graham's information was critical, maybe even the break she needed. But leaving again meant risking more distance with Renee, more questions that might not have easy answers.

"Okay," she said decisively. "I'll be there soon."

She hung up and reached for her coat again, feeling the echo of James's words in her mind: Just a chance is all I'm asking for. She knew she owed the same to Renée, but that chance with Graham felt like a deadline ticking away. Nicole grabbed the car keys and kissed Renée on her forehead before heading out: "Graham is ready to talk. I need to go now. Back soon. Love you."

The drive into the city was both familiar and foreign at this late hour, the roads mercifully empty compared to the chaos of her thoughts. She sped through intersections on yellow, watching the skyline loom closer and remembering when she first fell in love with it—the thrill of chasing stories through crowded streets, the sense of purpose and freedom. But now it was entangled with personal upheaval, a web of ambition and fear she couldn't seem to untangle.

Albert had texted an address near Union Station, where a cluster of seedy motels huddled together like conspirators.

Nicole parked around the corner, eyeing a group of teenagers who loitered by a boarded-up storefront. They watched her with disinterested curiosity as she hurried past.

Albert let her in through the back door, his expression one of practiced exasperation. "You took your sweet time," he chided, leading her up a narrow staircase that smelled faintly of mildew and stale cigarettes.

"I thought you wanted me to be discreet," Nicole shot back, trying to match his nonchalance even as nerves tightened in her stomach.

"Discreet, not invisible. If Graham gets antsy—"

The door at the end of the hall creaked open, and a figure emerged, pacing in agitation. "She's here," Albert called.

Graham looked even more harried than before, his eyes darting about the dim hallway like a trapped animal's. He disappeared back into the room, leaving the door ajar in a clear invitation to follow.

Nicole hesitated at the threshold, and Albert nudged her impatiently. "Go on, talk him down before he jumps."

Inside, Graham twisted his hands and scanned the windows nervously. "This place is crawling with cops," he insisted as soon as Nicole entered. "I'm getting out of here."

"Graham," she said firmly, closing the door behind her. "You're safe. Just sit and talk to me."

He sank into a chair reluctantly, but his foot tapped out his anxiety in a frantic rhythm against the floor. "I can smell them," he muttered, more to himself than to her.

Nicole crouched next to him, keeping her voice steady. "We're the only ones who know you're here. You can trust Albert. Now tell me what you've got before we both risk our necks for nothing."

Graham's eyes flicked towards her, full of distrust and desperation. She recognized the look—it was the same one she had seen on the rookie cop she'd interviewed, a man at the end of his rope.

"I've got names," he said finally, his voice thin and cracking. "Names of officers working with the dealers. But it's bigger than just that," he added quickly. "There's someone high up pulling strings."

"Someone?" Nicole pressed, feeling adrenaline sharpen her focus.

"The mayor," Graham said in a hushed tone, as though speaking it aloud would summon danger into the room.

Her heart leapt, confirming what she had suspected but couldn't yet prove. This was the lead she needed—the connection that could break the story wide open. "You're sure?" she asked, urgency infusing her words.

"I've seen them together," Graham insisted, his eyes wide with the revelation. "Meetings in places so public it makes you sick."

"You have to give me specifics," Nicole urged. "The who and the when—I need it all."

Graham hesitated, visibly torn between fear and a need to unburden himself. "I don't have it all here," he admitted, frustration lining his voice. "But I can get you more if—if I know I'm safe."

"You will be," Nicole promised with more conviction than she felt. "We'll keep you covered until this blows over."

He shot her a skeptical glance but continued anyway. "Tomorrow night," he said, his voice steadier now. "There's another meeting at the old pier. That's where they'll be."

Nicole took a mental note of the location, formulating a plan even as her pulse quickened with the enormity of what he was offering. "If you get me details, we can blow this open," she said, trying to convey urgency without panic.

Graham nodded, though doubt still flickered in his eyes. "I'll try," he said, his earlier bravado slipping.

Before Nicole could say more, Albert appeared at the door. "Time to scram," he announced brusquely. "We've risked enough for one night."

Graham bolted from his chair and past them both, his departure hasty and desperate. Nicole watched him go, wondering if she would see him again—or if fear would drive him too far underground this time.

"Think he'll come through?" Albert asked as they trailed Graham down the stairs.

"He has to," Nicole replied, hoping her confidence didn't sound as hollow to Albert as it did to her own ears.

They reached the street without noticing the black SUV that was observing them. James discreetly ensured the area was secure so Nicole's meeting with Albert and Graham would go undisturbed, having personally arranged the meeting through his security firm. Hacking into Albert's email had been straightforward; conveying his good intentions was the real challenge. James knew Graham was an informant, but so did the other criminals in the vicinity. If anyone else discovered Graham's activities, his life, along with those he contacted, would be in grave danger.

Nicole quickly returned to her vehicle, her thoughts racing as she processed Graham's revelations and the perilous new aspects they added to her story. The significance of his promises both excited and alarmed her. She failed to notice James, who remained hidden, maintaining a cautious distance as she drove away into the night.

After she left, James emerged from his hiding spot and made a phone call. "It's me," he said softly. "Yes, she met with him."

The next morning arrived with crisp, clear skies. Nicole stood at the kitchen counter, sipping a fresh cup of coffee, her resolve strengthened. She had investigated every possible lead but found no vulnerabilities in her security; whoever leaked Graham's information was meticulous and deliberate.

"Mom, I think the police followed me home yesterday," Noah said, anxiety evident in his voice. "I saw them while coming back from school, and as I got closer to our house, they drove off."

Nicole's grip on her cup tightened. "Did they speak to you?"

Noah shook his head, his eyes wide with a mix of fear and curiosity. "Just... watching."

Renée entered the room, assessed the situation, and sat down next to him. "Sweetie, are you sure it wasn't just a coincidence?"

He shrugged, uncertainty clouding his expression. "I don't know."

Nicole forced a reassuring smile, determined to keep him calm. "We'll figure it out," she said, gently ruffling his hair. But her mind was already racing.

She exchanged a glance with Renée, who nodded with silent understanding. "Hey, Noah," Renée said cheerfully, "how about I take you to the park later?" Your mom can finish her work and then join us."

His face brightened. "Can we bring Marley?" he asked eagerly.

"Of course," Renée laughed. "I'll get everything ready."

As Noah dashed up the stairs, Nicole exhaled slowly, her thoughts a chaotic mix of worry and potential scenarios. Being watched was troubling enough. But now Noah was noticing it too.

"I'll let you know if they come back," Renée murmured, giving Nicole's arm a reassuring squeeze. "Try not to worry."

Easier said than done, Nicole thought as she turned back to her laptop. The email stared back at her, taunting in its simplicity: a single ominous line sent just hours before her meeting with James.

"You're in over your head."

She took a deep breath and started typing, her fingers moving with urgency.

Nicole struggled to piece together how events had spiraled so suddenly. Her journalistic instincts told her she was missing a crucial puzzle piece, something that would connect Graham's paranoia with the threat looming over them. The message she received could be a warning—or a trap. Her thoughts kept returning to

James, wondering if he was playing an angle she hadn't yet seen.

Lost in her work, she hardly noticed the hours slipping by until Renée's voice interrupted her focus. "We're heading out now," Renée called from the hallway.

"Be careful," Nicole responded reflexively, not looking up from the screen.

Renée hesitated, then added softly, "Don't let this consume you."

Nicole glanced at her then, seeing the mix of concern and affection etched on Renée's face. "I won't," she promised, though both of them knew it was a lie.

The door closed behind Renée and Noah, leaving Nicole alone with the quiet hum of the house and the urgency of her investigation. She resolved to trace every lead, knowing it was the only way to protect her family from the growing danger.

The sun was low on the horizon when she last checked her phone, expecting a flurry of messages from Renée. But it remained silent, except for a voicemail notification from an unknown number. Her heart skipped as she played it.

"Listen carefully," the voice said, its tone altered and unidentifiable. "Stay away from the pier tonight. This is your one and only warning."

A cold fear settled over her. She called Renée's cell, but it went straight to voicemail. Panic started clawing at her resolve; she left a hasty message and tried to gather her thoughts.

Her instincts screamed for action, but she knew she needed to tread carefully. One misstep could put them all in danger—especially Noah. With mounting desperation, she grabbed her keys, ready to track down her family before anything could happen.

They sat in the van, watching Nicole frantically drive away from the house. Reynolds checked his phone, eyes scanning a text with a single name: Graham.

"She's leaving."

"Yeah, she's leaving, and it's your fault. If you hadn't followed the kid home, she would still be in the house right now."

"Blame me all you want, but none of this would've happened if you knew how to drive," Reynolds shot back, his voice tight with annoyance.

Carlos lit a cigarette and leaned back, the van's metal groaning beneath his weight. "We'll torch the place, just like we're supposed to. That'll get the message across."

Reynolds looked out at the empty street. "We should wait," he insisted. "See if they come back."

"No," Carlos said, biting off the word. "We do it now before anyone notices us hanging around again."

They moved quickly, slipping from the van and up the drive like shadows. The windows stared blankly at them as they circled the house with cans of gasoline in their hands. Reynolds kept glancing over his shoulder, nervous.

"Relax," Carlos sneered when they met up at the front steps.

They doused everything—the porch, the shrubs by the entryway—and then Carlos struck a match, tossing it with a flick of his wrist. Flames burst upwards, licking at the eaves as they hustled back to the van.

Reynolds climbed into the driver's seat, his hands trembling on the wheel. The fire caught in the rearview mirror, a bloom of orange and red, and he felt a sick twist of satisfaction. He started the engine. "What if someone sees?"

"Let them," Carlos said, slamming the door shut. "This is what we want."

Reynolds drove slowly at first, careful not to draw attention, then picked up speed as they turned out of the neighborhood. Silence settled between them, thick and tense, each lost in their own thoughts. Reynolds imagined Nicole seeing the house—or what was left of it—his mind flicking through images of rage and desperation.

Carlos exhaled smoke into the cramped air of the van. "She won't be able to run forever."

Reynolds nodded, though doubt nagged at him like an itch he couldn't reach. She had always been resourceful; she'd managed to stay out of sight for this long.

Impatience and Investigation

J ames sat in the leather chair staring at his phone. He'd resisted checking it every five minutes since their meeting, but impatience gnawed at him. Had he pushed too hard? Not enough?

Across from him sat his father, George Williams, a retired deputy and the only private investigator in Ashland, North Carolina. He didn't like being questioned as a grown man, especially in his own house, where there was always a hint of interrogation in his father's questioning that he found annoying.

Williams, a hard-nosed, old-school cop, had been one of Ashland's well-respected Black officers in the county for over thirty years. They were supposed to be two hundred miles south of Maryland, but they decided at the last minute to visit—which wasn't a surprise, since his family usually popped up unexpectedly at his home where he used to live in North Carolina.

He scrolled idly through emails, stopping when he reached the name Graham. Something about it tugged at a memory from long ago—a case his father had worked before retiring. He hesitated, then opened it, scanning the contents with growing interest.

"What's the problem?" George inquired, watching as James' face shifted expression.

"I'm not completely sure," James replied. He closed his email and set down his phone, trying to assemble a puzzle spinning in all directions.

"You seem preoccupied."

James let out a sharp exhale. "It's complicated."

George reclined in his chair, observing him. "Complicated, as in, with a woman?"

"Yeah," James conceded, rubbing the back of his neck. "Exactly, with a woman."

His father gave a knowing nod. "And this Nicole—is she the real reason you're staying?"

James hesitated, taken aback by how quickly George pinpointed the truth. "Partly," he answered carefully.

"I understand," George said softly, a rare tenderness in his tone. "Sometimes, letting go isn't the solution."

James met his father's gaze. "And sometimes, it really isn't."

George chuckled dryly. "You've always been obstinate." He rose and stretched. "Come on, let's grab a drink before we head back."

"It's too early for a beer, don't you think?"

"Absolutely not!" George snapped, seizing the bottle opener to quickly crack open two bottles. "This is a celebration. At last, I have a grandson from my little man. I couldn't be a happier Papa."

"I didn't think you'd be so excited given the circumstances," James remarked.

"Well, things could be better, but having a child to continue the Williams name is something to appreciate, if you ask me." George clarified, taking another hearty gulp before setting his bottle aside. James was pleased to catch his father in a good mood. At other times, his clear-sighted judgment would have spiraled into countless criticisms. "Have you told your mother yet? She's going to need a massive drink when she hears this."

"No, not yet. I was waiting for the right moment."

"Grace, come here. Now is as good a time as any, don't you think? When can we meet him?"

"I was just about to text his mother to see if she had plans this evening. I wanted to see him for a while."

There was some truth to that—but also the fact that he longed to see Nicole again. She was constantly on his mind. For some unexplainable reason, he yearned to feel her hair through his fingers. He recalled that it was thick and black as he watched her arranging decorations for Noah's birthday earlier that week. He'd captured its essence—a hint of vanilla—when she fell into his arms.

"We'll come with you, so you won't have to go there alone, son... son?"

James snapped out of his daydream just in time to catch the tail end of his father's question.

"Maybe it's too soon."

"Why not? We're family now, and we need to see my grandson. I always knew Grace should have packed my good shirt."

James began tapping away at his phone, hoping it wasn't too late and that she would reply promptly without dismissing the time.

How are you doing? I was really hoping Noah could come over tonight.

Send

I'm not sure; today might not be the best time.

Is everything alright?

Typing...

We had some issues come up today.

I'm here for you; I can help.

Typing... James could sense her reluctance.

Send the address. We'll be there in forty-five minutes.

James looked at the incoming message and smiled. "Nicole said it's fine to go see Noah."

"You want to let her know your family is here and that they want to see him too."

"Yes, I suppose I should mention I've got extra support with me."

"Funny."

"Maybe I should warn her first, so she'll be ready when they all arrive."

"Nonsense. Your mom can fix us all something to drink right now. And if her family is anything like ours, we'll all get along just fine."

James pondered those words carefully. If her family was indeed similar to his, they'd both end up needing headache medicine—and a stiff drink—for all the antics they were sure to bring along.

They drove through a world between dusk and dawn. The city's grime was gone. Instead, the air smelled of pine needles and distant rain. Shadows moved quickly, appearing and disappearing. Nicole gripped the steering wheel tightly. Raindrops fell on the windshield. They were left over from the earlier storm. It had forced them off the road. Time felt strange. Miles blurred together. Noah fell asleep. Renée stared out the window, silent.

"Mom, are we there?" Noah's voice, still heavy with sleep, emerged as he shifted in the back seat.

"We're here, sweetheart," Nicole replied, fighting to hide the fatigue in her tone.

Noah, rubbing his eyes, pressed his face to the window. "It looks huge."

Nicole and Renée stepped out of the car and paused at the threshold of the all-brick colonial, immediately struck by its timeless elegance. The sweeping circular driveway, flanked by arched windows and a paved flagstone pathway. As they ascended the path, every detail—from the stately exterior to the inviting door—crafted a scene of refined serenity, beckoning them inside.

"Wow," Noah exclaimed. "Does he have a dog?"

Nicole smiled, ruffling his hair. "Why don't you ask him yourself?"

The front door opened, and James emerged, wearing a broad, welcoming grin. His eyes found Nicole's and lingered, a moment of electricity arching between them.

Renée stepped back, folding her arms, watching the exchange with increasing annoyance.

"Hey, there!" James called, his focus shifting to Noah. "And who is this big guy?"

Noah hopped out of the car and ran toward him. "I'm here! I'm here!"

"You sure are, buddy!" James said, scooping him up with practiced ease.

Nicole approached, her steps cautious yet drawn by an invisible tether. "Thanks for having us," she said, a touch of uncertainty in her voice.

"Thank you for coming," James replied, the sincerity unmistakable. "I wasn't sure after..." "how things ended."

"Yeah," Nicole acknowledged softly, her gaze shifting to the ground. "Well, here we are."

James nodded, sensing her apprehension. "Come on inside. It's too cold to stand out here."

Once within, the home unfolded like a carefully composed masterpiece. The expansive two-story foyer, gleaming with the radiance of pristine porcelain tile floors, set the stage for what Nicole would soon learn was far more than just a beautiful house. In the living room, an elegant marble fireplace cast a warm glow, its flames leaping and casting playful shadows across the walls, hinting at the countless family stories etched in the flicker of its light. A generous dining room, promising evenings filled with laughter and soulful conversations, couldn't shake Nicole's thoughts of the father of her child. As she wandered through the home, her eyes were drawn to a spacious private office and a gourmet kitchen outfitted with quartz countertops and crisp white cabinetry. In that moment, her admiration for the home's intricate details yielded to the complexity of the man who had built this life.

This house was more than just a structure; it was a stage for interwoven narratives of relationships and hidden secrets. Her heart quickened at the thought of meeting his parents—a vital, yet daunting, milestone in her uncertain journey.

Before long, in the elegantly appointed living area, she found herself face-to-face with them.

Noah bounced on his toes, unmistakably exuberant as he waved, "Hi!" His voice cut through the atmosphere with refreshingly candid enthusiasm.

"Welcome," his mother greeted warmly, her tone both kind and cautiously measured. She moved with deliberate ease as she carried a freshly baked sweet potato pie, ready to serve. Beneath the surface, however, the delight in James's expression couldn't completely disguise the nervousness as he registered their arrival.

"Didn't expect you this soon," James remarked, his voice too controlled to hide the unspoken truth. Nicole's presence clearly stirred emotions in him that he struggled to articulate—a blend of reassurance and overwhelming sentiment.

James' father was acutely aware of the emotional and strategic stakes at play. He watched as his wife placed the pie on the table and offered Noah a welcoming smile, then shifted her observant eyes around the room, as if absorbing every detail.

"You must be Nicole and Renée," he said, each name carrying weight as he regarded both women before glancing over at James.

Nicole adjusted her blouse, maintaining a composed expression that belied the inner adjustments happening beneath. She embraced Noah's grandmother briefly and nodded approvingly at the pie. "That smells wonderful."

"We just couldn't wait," Grace added in a tone that blended diplomacy with genuine warmth, her eyes lingering fondly on Noah, whose vibrant energy filled the room. "We've heard so much about you."

His grandfather then offered a firm yet gentle welcome: "It's a pleasure to finally meet you."

"We've been looking forward to this for a while," Grace continued, still casting affectionate glances at Noah.

"And you must be Noah."

A silent understanding passed between James and George as they exchanged a look—each silently acknowledging the surprises and adjustments that now lay ahead, even if their visions had not entirely aligned.

Never missing a beat, Noah announced, "I'm Noah," as if declaring it to a grand audience, his delighted tone infusing the room with excitement.

"Isn't he the spitting image?" George observed warmly, his words carrying both genuine affection and an undercurrent of strategic meaning.

James nodded, his thoughts racing in multiple directions as he sensed the shifting dynamics brought on by the integration of his new life with his family's past. The Winn family was now adjusting to this influx of new energy, new personalities orbiting around an old, familiar center.

They moved into the living room, where the comforting presence of Noah mingled with a newfound tension among the expanded family. Ornate vases and carefully arranged plants formed a subtle barrier around the mantel, behind which a framed family photo—with James, his father, mother, and sisters—reminded everyone of the life that existed before Nicole, Renée, and Noah arrived.

Grace and George exchanged looks with practiced precision, a silent conversation conveyed through every glance and movement. They arranged their suitcases near the couch, creating an impromptu nesting area for themselves. Despite their assured demeanor, both knew they were treading on delicate ground that demanded more than simple confidence.

"I suppose we've got quite a lot to work through," James mused, breaking the silence and acknowledging the intricate dance unfolding before them.

"You're not wrong," George replied with a familiar pat on James's back, exuding a mix of paternal care and camaraderie.

Noah quickly darted back to James's side, as if determined to keep his small world intact and avoid any potential separations. Watching him, Renée's eyes softened, and she let her guard drop for a brief moment at the pure, unbridled enthusiasm he displayed.

"So many people to get to know," Grace remarked with a spark of anticipation as she joined George near the mantel.

"As long as it isn't too many all at once," Nicole quipped with a smile that conveyed both welcome and the boundaries they still needed to enforce.

"How about dinner for the troops?" Grace suggested, injecting a touch of levity into the tense, reformed constellation of their household. "I think we could feed an army tonight."

George looked at her with admiration. "Smart to be prepared," he said. "Always good to know what you're up against."

The remark drew soft laughs from the group, puncturing the lingering tension with hints of humor and normalcy. Slowly, as everyone eased into the living area, tentative conversations began to blossom. George engaged Noah in chat about school, his questions gentle probes into the boy's young life. Meanwhile, Grace and

Nicole discovered common ground in work and shared projects; their conversations were careful yet revealing more than they had intended. Renée, ever the observer, listened intently, cataloging details in preparation for whatever might come next.

James felt both a part of the scene and strangely apart from it as he navigated his evolving place within a family that was not yet entirely his but held endless possibilities for the future. In a fleeting moment, he caught Noah's eyes—a small but certain connection amid so many uncertainties.

Above them all, the family photo on the mantel stood as a testament to a bygone era, now temporarily set aside for this burgeoning, more crowded gathering. Everyone present was aware of the changes that night heralded and how much, in time, the picture of their lives would be rewritten.

As the evening wound to a close and the last of the pie disappeared, Noah's energy eventually gave way to sleepiness. His eyelids fluttered like moths before he curled up on the couch, Renée's sweater as his makeshift blanket. Nicole watched him with a protective tenderness that couldn't mask her own exhaustion. "We should get going," she mentioned, uncertainty creeping into her voice as she considered the drive ahead. Grace, perceptive and quick, offered a warm and insistent alternative. "Nonsense. We have plenty of room. Stay the night." She exchanged a look with George, who nodded approvingly. "We insist." Nicole hesitated. It was a large step, more than she'd expected, more than she'd prepared for. But Noah's peaceful breathing and the appealing warmth of the house lured her toward acceptance.

The words caught in Nicole's throat, the prospects overwhelming and inviting all at once. But before she could decide, before the night could settle into this new shape, Renée's phone erupted into a shrill ring, cutting through the room and bringing an abrupt halt to the conversations. She answered quickly, her expression tightening with each word. Her voice, when it returned, was laced with urgency and dread. "Our house—it's on fire."

The declaration sent shockwaves through the room, replacing the tentative warmth with immediate alarm. Nicole looked at her, stricken. "What? How?"

"Neighbors called," Renée managed, the phone still clutched in her hand like a live wire. "We have to go."

The words were barely finished before Nicole was gathering their things with frantic energy, her mind already miles away, racing toward the endangered home.

James didn't hesitate. "We're coming with you," he declared, the decisive tone leaving no room for argument. The household transformed from idle conversation to organized chaos, each movement precise and driven by a singular urgency. George slipped into old habits, coordinating the exit with a practiced calm. "I'll call the station and get them to send extra units," he assured Nicole and Renée, understanding the importance of immediate action.

Grace picked up Noah, who was already stirring at the commotion, and wrapped James's jacket around him. "Stay safe," she urged as she handed him over, her voice steady yet filled with concern.

"Thanks for everything," Nicole said, her voice choked with gratitude and anxiety. She turned to follow James out the door, her steps quickened by the gravity of the situation.

As they piled into the car, the engine roared to life, and they sped into the night, leaving the warmth and security of the house behind. The road unfolded before them, each mile laden with tension and expectation. Nicole sat in the back with Noah, who was now fully awake and sensing the urgency, peppering her with questions she struggled to answer. Renée twisted around from the front seat, her eyes wide with worry as she scanned the horizon for any hint of their neighborhood.

James drove with singular focus, his hands tight on the wheel as he navigated the darkened streets. The world outside became a blur of streetlights and shadows, each flicker adding to the mounting dread. For a moment, he glanced back at Nicole, their eyes meeting in a silent exchange of fear and determination. "We'll get there," he promised, his voice firm against the rising panic.

Nicole nodded, clutching Noah close. Her mind raced through a thousand scenarios, each one more frightening than the last. She fought to maintain composure, to offer reassurance when her own foundations felt so abruptly shaken.

The drive stretched into a tense eternity until the unmistakable glow of emergency lights appeared in the distance. The scene was chaos—flashing lights from emergency vehicles painted harsh stripes across the street, while firefighters hurried to contain the smoldering wreckage.

Before they could even exit the car, the fire chief waved them back with urgent gestures, his shouts barely cutting through the cacophony of crackling embers and shouting voices. "Stay back! It's too dangerous!" The sight pierced through Nicole, leaving her breathless and shaky.

Renée gasped, her hand over her mouth, as they skidded to a stop outside the fenced perimeter. "Oh my God," she whispered, the reality sinking in. "We're too late."

Nicole stumbled out of the car, eyes locked on what remained of her house. "Our house..." Her voice broke over the words, a raw sound swallowed by the night air.

James quickly pulled Noah to his side, urging him to remain nearby as he hurried over to Nicole, his expression a blend of shock and worry.

"Everything's gone," Nicole whispered, her gaze fixed on the ashes still glowing with heat.

The fire chief approached them cautiously, looking weary but determined. "We're doing everything we can to figure out what happened," he said. "Could have been a gas leak, but it's too early to say for sure. Neighbors across the street had spotted thick, black smoke snaking out of the second-story window.

"Two men had run from the house and got into a black SUV." A neighbor chimed in.

James put an arm around Nicole, pulling her close. "Is there anything I can do? Anywhere you need me to be?"

Nicole blinked back tears, trying to regain composure. "I don't even know where to start..."

James stepped forward, his voice gentle but firm. "Why don't we get you all out of here? You can stay with us tonight."

"Thank you," Nicole murmured, her voice barely above a whisper.

"Come on," James said, guiding her toward the car. "We'll figure everything out tomorrow."

As they drove away, Nicole's eyes stayed glued to the rearview mirror, to the place where her life had once stood solid and whole.

She sat stiffly in the backseat, her silence a thick, palpable thing. James tried to fill it with cheerful chatter. "We've got plenty of space. We'll make up the guest rooms for you, Renée, and Noah!"

Renée turned around from the front seat, her usual sarcasm absent. "Are you sure you're ready for us again so soon?"

James gave her a reassuring nod, but his mind was already racing ahead to the logistics. "Absolutely. It'll be like a sleepover," he added, taking a swift turn and heading back through the maze of streets they'd just traveled.

He dug his phone from his pocket and quickly dialed, anticipation threading his voice. "Mom. We're bringing them back."

The line was quiet for a beat, then Grace's voice came through, calm but edged with surprise. "Is everyone alright?"

Yeah, we're fine," James replied. "But it's been a night."

"Let us know when you're close," Grace instructed. "We'll have everything ready."

The call ended, and the silence returned, heavier now but somehow shared. Nicole watched the road with eyes that seemed to absorb every shadow and light, as if each passing moment could bring another unforeseen shift.

"Noah, how are you doing back there?" James asked, glancing in the mirror.

The boy clutched his action figure, his grip as tight as his voice. "Okay, I guess."

Nicole reached over, stroking his hair. "It's just for a little while, sweetheart."

A strange calm settled over her as they neared the house for the second time that evening. She couldn't yet untangle the mess of emotions and uncertainty, but a small part of her felt a flicker of relief. Maybe being with James and his family could offer them more than just shelter.

They arrived at last, and this time James's parents greeted them with a prepared house and open arms. Heavy coats were quickly taken and hung, towels handed out, and warm hugs exchanged with firm assurances that they'd be alright.

Grace led them back into the living room, where the fireplace whispered comfort into the chilly night. She beckoned them to sit, then vanished into the kitchen, returning with hot chocolate and snacks in a display of maternal precision.

"Drink up," she insisted gently. "You'll feel better."

Nicole nodded, accepting the mug with a grateful if tremulous smile. Her exhaustion weighed heavily, but the room's warmth and the family's easy camaraderie began to thaw the shock that had gripped her all night.

"We can talk about next steps in the morning," James said, sitting beside her with a quiet confidence that offered unexpected comfort.

Noah, still clutching his action figure, looked around at the attentive faces, slowly relaxing into the novelty of being surrounded by so many people. "Can I sleep in there?" he asked, pointing to the couch nearest the fireplace.

Grace chuckled, smoothing the hair off his forehead. "Anywhere you like, sweetheart."

Renée sat cross-legged on the floor, leaning against the sofa with a sigh of relief. "I didn't think we'd be back here so soon."

"Guess we didn't scare you away, after all," James quipped, savoring the chance to lighten the mood.

Nicole shot him a grateful glance, then turned her attention to Noah, who'd already stretched out and tucked himself into a cozy ball.

"Couldn't keep us away if we tried," Renée chimed in, her eyes meeting Nicole's for a brief, unguarded moment.

James's mom led Nicole and Renée upstairs, fussing over pillows and blankets like she was swaddling a child.

"There," she said with a satisfied smile. "This should be nice and cozy."

Nicole stood awkwardly by the door. "You really don't have to do all this."

"Nonsense." James's mom waved her off, oblivious to Nicole's discomfort. "You just make yourself at home."

Once she left, Nicole sank onto the bed. Renée started her nightly shower routine without pause for the evening's events. The room was quiet now, dimly lit by the glow of a nightlight plugged into the wall. Nicole stared up at the ceiling, trying to resist the pull of her thoughts—who would have run from the house? And why? All those memories, all those pieces of their lives. Her eyes drifted to the window, where the night pressed in with a suffocating weight.

She rolled over, pulling a pillow tightly to her chest, its scent foreign and comforting all at once.

There was a soft knock on the door, and James slipped in quietly. "Hey," he said, his voice low and careful. "Are you okay? Can I come in?"

"Yeah," Nicole replied, her voice barely carrying. She glanced at the bathroom door. Renée still hadn't emerged yet.

"Listen," James said, sitting beside her. "I know it feels overwhelming right now. But I'm here for you. We'll fix this."

She wanted to believe him, wanted to take comfort in his words. But doubt gnawed at her, relentless and cruel.

"Did you hear what that woman said?" Nicole asked, her voice suddenly sharp with urgency. "Two men ran from the house. What if... what if it wasn't an accident?"

James looked startled, taken aback by the accusation hanging in the air. "You think someone did this on purpose?"

"Yes, I do," she admitted, frustration edging her words. "But it doesn't make sense otherwise."

James was silent for a moment, processing. "Okay," he finally said, his expression turning determined. "Then we find out who did this. We don't give them the satisfaction of thinking they've won."

His resolve was comforting, a small anchor in the chaos. Nicole nodded, feeling a flicker of strength return. She took a deep breath, willing herself to be brave.

"Get some sleep," James urged gently. "Tomorrow, we'll get some answers."

He brushed a kiss across her forehead and slipped out of the room, leaving her alone with her thoughts once more. Nicole lay still, letting the silent stretch throughout the room like an unspoken promise. Eventually, exhaustion pulled at her eyelids, and she drifted

into a restless sleep filled with flickering images of fire
and smoke.

Nicole woke to the darkness pressing close, the air thick
with night's uncertainty. Her phone lit up, the screen
flashing with a message from James: I'm outside. Come
down?

She quietly removed the covers and put on her
shoes, making sure not to disturb Renée. The house was
enveloped in the profound silence that comes only at 3
a.m. She navigated through it with a careful urgency, her
anxious fingers lightly touching the stair railing.

When she stepped outside, the cold hit her first, a
slap of reality. James was leaning against his car, hands
stuffed in his pockets, his silhouette a familiar comfort.
He looked up as she approached, and she could see the
worry etched in his eyes.

"Couldn't sleep?" he asked, pulling her into a hug
that dissolved the chill between them.

"Not really," Nicole murmured into his shoulder,
feeling the knot inside her loosen a fraction. "You neither?"

"Figured you might need company," he said, resting his chin against her hair. They stood like that for a

minute or two, letting the silence work its way around them. The world was an immense, quiet space, and they were the only two people in it.

"How are you doing? Really?" James asked, pulling back just enough to see her face.

"I don't know," Nicole admitted, her voice a fragile thing. "I keep replaying it, wondering how... why it happened."

"We'll figure it out," he reassured, the words solid and unyielding. "I'll talk to my dad first thing. We'll get to the bottom of this."

Nicole nodded, but the questions still gnawed at her, sharp and relentless. "What if it was someone trying to scare us? To run us out of town?"

James's expression darkened, his jaw set. "Then they picked the wrong people to mess with."

A breath of laughter escaped her, unexpected but welcome. "You probably love this. Another case to solve."

"Maybe." He cracked a smile, the tension lifting for a moment. "Guess I'm still my father's son."

Nicole tucked herself closer against him, the warmth of his body a balm against her frayed nerves.

"Thank you. For being here."

"Where else would I be?" he murmured softly, pressing a tender kiss on her hair, a gentle promise sealed between them. They lingered beneath the expansive, indifferent sky, holding onto each other as if the world might disappear. But as the chill began to creep through the warmth, Nicole shivered in her thin sweater, feeling the cold not just in the air but somewhere deeper. "Let's get you inside," James suggested, his voice a soothing balm as he rubbed her arms with affection, guiding her gently towards the door. Once back in the guest room, she found Renée nestled under the covers, her steady breathing a lullaby in the quiet room. Nicole slipped out of her shoes and slid under the blanket, seeking solace in sleep yet feeling a strange distance, hoping for rest without the intrusion of dreams that might betray her heart.

The drawstring to her pajamas loosened.

Within seconds she felt his warm fingers reach inside. Nicole's eyes snapped open immediately, and she glanced around. She must've dozed off on the chair beside the bedroom window. Renée was sound asleep. Someone was over her shoulders.

James.

Wet lips slid down the top of her ear to her neck, and soon she lost focus on his skilled hands beneath her pants. He used his mouth in a way that ignited the increasing warmth between her legs. A feeling she had never felt before.

Within seconds he had her so aroused she slid out of his grasp and stood, letting her pants fall to the floor. She looked at him with curious eyes.

"Come with me," she said, bringing him to his full height, her voice filled with eager emotion. She held his hand, leading him to the bathroom before turning around and slowly closing the door behind her to not disturb the sleeping spouse inches from where they stood. He positioned her against the sink.

"Take your top off," he told her.

As she slipped her t-shirt off, he kissed the tops of her breasts and massaged her inner thighs before pulling her underwear down over her feet.

Her breathing became labored. "I've never been with a man before."

He bent down to a knee position and picked her up gently, forearms under her bottom. Her hands immediately grasped both sides of the sink for balance, but she knew he wouldn't let her fall.

"I've wanted to taste you for so long," he said. His mouth kissed her vagina before his tongue took over, delving into the deepest parts of her.

He rolled his tongue against her clitoris, dipping in and out until it changed direction to explore her opening. Her whole body became undone, and she could barely contain the moans that escaped from her lips.

Everything he did, her body answered with a need she'd never known before. The attention he paid to her, coupled with her desire for him, made her wonder why he had begun this. But her hands had been busy, and he was getting beyond the point where he cared about these mixed messages. She whispered things in his ear, rude and encouraging things.

He held her tight, thrusting against her stomach, energy concentrated on the powerful electricity coursing through his genitals. And then he felt himself lose control.

Release flooded him, and with it the familiar depletion. Emptiness. Desperation. The all-consuming need for blood.

She collapsed into his arms, clutching onto him like a child, crying soundlessly. Startled, he held her without understanding what was going on. She seemed beyond consolation, and he found that disturbing. But intuition assured him that he had just learned something about her, something important. If only, he thought, I could make sense of this girl.

The shout from her orgasm awakened both her and Renée.

"Nicole, are you okay?"

"Yeah, just a dream. Go back to sleep."

Morning
Clarity

The morning came too soon, with sunlight slicing through the window.

Nicole lay curled under the covers, shadows clinging to her like a second skin. Her mind churned with images of smoke and ash, restlessly replaying every detail. She finally slipped from bed, moving quietly to avoid waking James.

Downstairs, the scent of coffee hung in the air, a whisper of normalcy in the chaos. James's mom, Grace, bustled around the kitchen. Her presence was warm, reassuring against Nicole's frayed nerves.

"Morning, sweetheart," Grace said softly. "I was just about to bring you a cup."

Nicole managed a grateful smile as she took the mug. "Thank you for letting us stay... I know it's sudden."

Grace dismissed her apologies with a wave. "You're family. You stay as long as you need." She paused, eyes full of concern. "Any word yet from the police?"

Nicole shook her head, worry knotting in her chest. "They said they'd call if they found anything. Where's Renée? Is Noah still asleep?"

James appeared, looking rumpled but ready. "They're with my father. Hey," he said, wrapping an arm around Nicole's waist. "You sleep, okay?"

"Not really." She leaned into him, grateful for his steady presence.

"Why don't you sit down?" Grace suggested. "I'll make some breakfast."

"No, really, you don't have to—" Nicole started, but Grace was already pulling out eggs and bread.

James led her to the table while his dad shuffled in with a newspaper, his expression grave. "Just heard on the radio," he announced. "They're saying it might have been arson."

Nicole's breath caught. "Arson?"

"Looks like it," he replied, gesturing to the stack of pancakes Grace placed before him.

Grace shot him a silencing look, then turned to Nicole with a softer expression.

"Whatever you need," James's mom added. "We're all here for you."

Nicole looked around at their expectant faces, feeling as though she stood at the edge of a cliff, unsure whether to leap or retreat. She swallowed hard, pushing past the confusion swirling inside. "I think we should focus on the fire," she said, her voice firming. "I'll go back to the house and see what the police know."

"Nicole—" James started, concern edging his tone.

"I just need to keep busy, okay?" She cut him off, a little too sharply. The press of their closeness was too much, and she needed air.

A silence followed, heavy with unspoken words. Finally, James nodded. "I'll go with you."

Renée stepped forward, her eyes searching Nicole's face. "I'll watch Noah."

Nicole smiled, grateful for the excuse to move, to escape the feelings she couldn't quite name. She picked up her shoes and coat and hurried to the car, James close behind.

The drive back to the house was tinged with a tense quiet, the morning sky a muted gray. James kept his eyes on the road, navigating the familiar turns with determined precision. Nicole stared out the window, the world blurring past like the fragments of the life she was trying to piece together.

When they arrived, the scene was far less chaotic. The street was lined with yellow tape, and smoke twisted lazily into the air from the charred remains. Only a few emergency vehicles remained, their lights a subdued pulse against the dull morning.

They parked and approached cautiously. A police officer stepped forward, recognizing Nicole from the night before. "Ma'am," he said with a nod. "We were hoping you'd come by."

Nicole's heart leaped. "Did you find anything?"

He gestured toward the house. "We're treating it as arson. Whoever did this knew what they were doing. The fire started around midnight in the living room. No sign of forced entry. Neighbors saw two men, like you said."

"Do you know who they were?" James asked, his voice firm.

"Not yet." The officer's tone was carefully measured, as if trying to bind all that was unknown into something he could tie down. "We'll need to ask you some questions later today."

Nicole nodded numbly, feeling the enormity of it all pressing down on her.

"Can we see the house?" James asked, his arm tightening protectively around Nicole.

"Not right now," the officer replied. "Too dangerous with the structure compromised."

James steered Nicole back toward the car gently. She moved as if through water, everything slowed and distorted by the weight of loss. Sitting in the passenger seat, she stared at her hands, which felt empty, useless against this sudden unraveling.

"Where should we go?" James asked as he started the engine. His voice was soft, tentative.

Nicole swallowed hard, trying to push words past the tightness in her throat. "I don't know... I just need to do something."

"We could get a coffee," James suggested. "Get away for a bit."

It seemed pointless, but so did everything else right now. "Okay," she agreed, willing herself to keep moving, to not get swallowed by the enormity of what was happening.

They drove in silence, Nicole's thoughts a tangled mess of anger and disbelief. Who would do this? Why? They pulled into a small café; windows fogged with warmth and chatter. A bell tinkled above the door as they entered, and Nicole flinched at how normal everything felt on this day that was anything but.

James ordered for both of them, coaxing a tight smile from Nicole. They settled at a small table by the window, the world outside blurred by steam and distance.

"This was personal, related to the story I'm investigating." Nicole asked abruptly, her eyes searching James's face for answers he didn't have.

He hesitated, choosing his words carefully. "Do you have an idea of who it could be?"

"I can narrow it down to a few," Nicole insisted, frustration threading through her voice. "Two men—"

"Hey," James interrupted gently, reaching across the table to take her hand. "We'll figure it out. I promise."

She wanted to believe him, to trust that their plans and dreams she had for her family hadn't gone up in flames along with the house. But doubt lingered, a stubborn shadow at the edge of every thought.

Their coffees arrived, and they sat in silence, the noise of the café a muffled hum around them.

Nicole finally spoke, her voice quieter now. "What if we never find out who did this?"

"We will," James said, with a certainty she wished she felt. "And even if it's not right away, I'll be with you every step."

The conviction in his voice was a lifeline, pulling her briefly above the storm of uncertainty. She nodded, squeezing his hand.

They left the café, the brightness of midday jarring against their dark thoughts. Nicole's phone buzzed as they reached the car. She glanced at the screen and felt her stomach twist.

"It's my dad," she said, showing the missed call to James.

"Do you want to call back now?" he asked, pausing with a hand on the door.

Nicole hesitated. How would she explain all of this? The fire, the suspicion, the fact that she didn't know what came next? She shook her head slowly. "Not yet."

"Okay," James said carefully, though worry flickered in his eyes.

They drove back to James's house under a sky that felt far too open, every mile bringing them closer to questions that loomed larger than the answers they hoped to find. Grace met them at the door, her expression a mix of relief and concern.

"Any news?" she asked, taking in their strained faces.

Nicole shook her head, feeling exhaustion sweep over her. "Just more questions."

Grace enveloped Nicole in a maternal hug, solid and comforting. "I hate seeing you go through this," she murmured.

James touched Nicole's arm lightly. "I'll get the phone charger from the car," he said, stepping back outside.

Nicole followed Grace into the living room, its warmth a jarring contrast to the cold chaos still swirling within her. She sank onto the couch, feeling the last of her energy ebb away.

"I made some chicken soup," Grace announced, bustling into the kitchen. "It's not much, but I figured you could use something hot."

Nicole nodded absently, staring at a photo on the mantel—James as a boy, grinning wide against a backdrop of mountains. A life built so carefully, piece by piece. Hers felt like it had slipped away, leaving nothing but smoke and questions.

Grace returned with a steaming bowl, pressing it into Nicole's hands. "I know you've got a lot on your mind," she said, her voice gentle. "But you need to keep your strength up."

"Thank you," Nicole whispered, though the food seemed foreign in her mouth. She ate a few spoonfuls out of politeness.

James reappeared with the charger, his expression softening when he saw her trying to eat. "You should rest," he suggested, sitting beside her.

"It's all I've been doing," Nicole replied, frustration creeping in again.

"Sometimes that's the only thing that helps," Grace said knowingly.

Nicole forced another smile and set the bowl down, untasted. "I'll try," she promised, more to placate his mother.

James didn't argue, just sat beside her and turned on the TV, flipping through channels aimlessly. He stopped on a nature documentary, its soothing narration a balm against the tension thickening the air.

Nicole leaned against James, feeling his steady heartbeat under her cheek.

The rhythmic thud was soothing, like the slow roll of waves against sand. She was comforted by his strength and something else she couldn't put her finger on. Thankful he was there, she closed her eyes, letting herself sink into the momentary peace. He turned towards her with such tenderness that it surprised her, and when his lips brushed her forehead, she felt a tremor run through her. It startled her how much she wanted him to do it again.

She shifted slightly, pulling back to see his face. "I don't know what I'd do without you," she said, her voice barely above a whisper.

"You won't have to find out," James replied, his eyes holding hers with an intensity that made her heart skip.

For a brief moment, everything else fell away—the fire, the questions, the gnawing uncertainty.

The front door opened with a clatter, breaking the spell. James's dad walked in briskly, clutching a plastic bag, with Noah and Renée following behind him.

Nicole sat up, blinking away the sudden intrusion. Her son's face was a mix of relief and worry. "Mom, Grandpa brought us some clothes." Noah said, dropping the duffel bag onto the floor. His voice sounded small in the large room. "Are we going to be okay?"

She pulled him close, feeling his warmth against her. "Of course we are," she said, trying to sound convincing.

Renée stood by the door, uncertainty flickering across her face. "I told him you needed space, but he wouldn't listen."

James exchanged a look with Nicole that was both knowing and amused. She squeezed his hand before reaching for Renée. "I'm glad you're here," she insisted, drawing her into a hug.

"James's father offered for us to stay here for a while..." Renée started, then trailed off, unable to finish the thought.

James's dad held up the bag triumphantly. "We brought some things from the store down the street. I figured you might need them." His cheerfulness was forced, a mask barely concealing his own anxiety.

"Thanks," Nicole replied, grateful even as she felt guilt twist inside her for worrying them.

The following weeks passed in a blur of makeshift routines. Grace and George had reluctantly returned to North Carolina, leaving the house feeling vast and empty even with all four of them there. Noah settled into a new school nearby, his resilience both a comfort and a reminder of how much Nicole had to hold together for his sake.

James and Renée threw themselves into work. Nicole, too, absorbed herself in her reporting, though each word she wrote felt miles away from where her thoughts truly lingered. They occasionally heard from the police, but never anything concrete—investigation ongoing, follow-up needed. It was infuriatingly vague, just like everything else in their lives right now.

At night, when exhaustion pulled heavily at her, Nicole would lie awake listening to the creaks of the unfamiliar house. She'd remember James's hand on hers or the way his eyes held hers with such certainty. The guilt tasted bitter; she tried to swallow it down but found it harder each day.

James would find her in the mornings, sitting at the kitchen table with coffee growing cold in front of her. He'd wrap her in a hug, whispering reassurances she tried to believe. She felt them drifting into new territories, where comfort blurred into something deeper, more complicated. She didn't know how to navigate this landscape, how to be thankful and aching all at once.

One night, when the house was finally quiet, Nicole slipped out of bed and found James on the back porch. He was leaning against the railing, staring up at the clear night sky. The air was crisp, biting at her skin as she joined him.

"Couldn't sleep?" he asked without looking over.

Nicole shook her head, folding her arms against the chill. "All I do is think." She paused, choosing her words carefully. "About everything."

James turned to face her then, his expression open and searching. "And?"

"And I don't know where I belong anymore," she admitted, her voice small against the vastness of the night.

James took a step closer, his presence warm in the cold air. "You belong right here," he said, his breath visible in the chill. "With me."

"Do I?" Nicole asked, fear threading her words. It was a question she hadn't dared to voice until now.

"Yes." He said it so simply, so surely, that Nicole felt something shift inside her.

They stood there for a moment, the silence between them deeper than words. And when James finally pulled her in, she let herself relax into him, letting go of everything except this one certain thing she felt him pull her even closer. His lips found her forehead, lingering there before moving to her cheek, each kiss a question she wasn't ready to answer. He paused just short of her mouth, and she pulled away abruptly, startled by how much she wanted him to continue.

Their eyes locked, an unspoken understanding passing between them.

"James, I—" Nicole began, then faltered. She backed away slowly, feeling the cold air where his warmth had been.

James watched as she retreated into the house, his expression one of longing and quiet resolve.

She closed the door gently behind her, leaning against it while trying to catch her breath. The room was dim and silent, a stark contrast to the noise in her head. She could still feel where his lips had touched her skin.

Upstairs, Noah was already asleep under layers of blankets. She watched him for a moment before slipping into bed beside Renee.

"Everything okay?" Renée murmured sleepily, turning toward her.

Nicole hesitated, words catching in her throat. "Yeah," she lied softly, staring into the dark. "Everything's fine."

Renée nodded, already drifting back to sleep. Nicole lay still, staring at the ceiling. She replayed the moment on the porch over and over; each memory a mix of guilt and yearning that kept her eyes open long into the night.

The next morning brought light that felt less harsh somehow, and Nicole woke with a tentative sense of clarity. She got Noah ready for school, tying up loose shoelaces and packing lunches with an energy she hadn't felt in weeks.

At breakfast, Renée studied her from across the table. "You seem different today," she remarked.

Nicole met her gaze evenly.

"Maybe I am," she replied, surprising herself with how true it felt.

She dropped Noah off at school and drove to James's office, feeling each mile bring her closer to something she wasn't sure how to name. Her heart thudded in her chest as she walked through the building, her resolve stronger than it had been in days.

James looked up from his desk when she entered, surprise melting into a smile. "Hey," he said cautiously. "Is everything—"

"I'm sorry about last night," Nicole interrupted, taking a step toward him. "I shouldn't have left like that."

James stood, closing the space between them. "You've got nothing to apologize for," he said gently.

"But I do." She took a deep breath, wanting him to understand. "I keep running because I'm scared of what all this means."

"And what does it mean?" James asked, his voice careful but hopeful.

"That I need you," Nicole admitted, her words trembling slightly. "More than I ever thought possible."

James's expression softened, a mix of relief and something more profound. He reached for her hand, pulling her closer. "We'll figure it out," he promised, his voice steady and sure.

Nicole nodded, feeling the warmth of his certainty seep into her. She rested her head against his chest, letting the moment stretch between them like a fragile truce.

They stayed that way until Nicole finally pulled back, feeling lighter than she had in weeks. "I should get going," she said reluctantly. "But... I just needed you to know."

James kissed her cheek, letting his lips linger with an unspoken promise of more to come. "I'm glad you decided to stay here with me."

She left his office with her heart still racing, each beat a reminder of what she'd found—and what she might lose if she wasn't careful.

The rest of the day unfolded with surprising ease. She wrote with new focus and clarity, her words sharp, and just when she thought her day couldn't get any better, the shrill ring of her phone pierced the silence.

She grabbed it quickly, hoping it was James on the other end. The display showed an unknown number, and something like hope flared up inside her.

"Hello?"

There was a pause on the line before a woman's voice spoke, low and deliberate. "You're too close. Back off now before it gets worse."

Static crackled briefly, and then the call cut out, leaving Nicole with the hollow echo of her own racing pulse. She stood frozen, the threat hanging in the air.

It took a moment for her to steady herself enough to call James.

He answered on the first ring. "Hey, I was just—"

"They called me," Nicole interrupted, her voice shaky but urgent. "They have my work phone. What if they find me again?"

James was silent for a beat, then his voice came through, strong and reassuring. "I'm coming to you right now. Don't go anywhere. We'll figure it out together."

Nicole nodded even though he couldn't see her, clutching the phone tighter as if it were an anchor. "Okay," she breathed.

She paced the room until she heard his knock at the door, her heart unspooling with relief as she let him in.

"Did you recognize the voice?" James asked immediately, concern etched across his face.

"No." Nicole shook her head, frustration mingling with fear.

"Whoever it was, they know about the story." She paused, her mind racing. "I should call Rodney."

James nodded, his hand on her shoulder.

She dialed quickly, her voice urgent when he picked up. "Rodney, it's Nicole. They know we're close."

"I figured," Rodney replied, his tone unsurprised but concerned. "What happened?"

"It was a warning, a woman's voice," she said, glancing at James. "Can you come to the house? Just make sure no one's following you."

"On my way," he assured, the line going dead.

Nicole turned to James, anxiety replacing her earlier relief. "What if they don't stop?"

"I won't let anything happen to you," James said, pulling her close. The determination in his voice was a lifeline she clung to.

They waited tensely until the doorbell rang. Rodney stood there, scanning the quiet street behind him before stepping inside quickly. "You sure it was a woman's voice, because sometimes you just don't know nowadays?" he asked flippantly.

Nicole nodded, a chill still clinging to her. "They said I'm too close."

Rodney rubbed his chin, thinking. "We should go through everything we've got on this story," he suggested. "See if there's something we missed."

James glanced at Nicole, then back at Rodney. "Do you know who might have the guts to do this?"

"I have some ideas," Rodney replied grimly. "Hell of a way to find out we're onto something big."

Nicole sat down heavily, her mind spinning. She felt James's hand on her back, grounding her amidst the chaos. "We can't stop now," she said with more conviction than she felt.

"Damn right we can't," Rodney agreed, reaching for his laptop. "Let's get to work."

They spread out notes and files across the table, piecing together the fragments of information they'd collected over weeks of research. Nicole's heart pounded as she read through each page, hoping for a clue that would make sense of the threat.

"What about this?" James asked, pointing to a grainy photo clipped to an article draft. It showed two men leaning against a black SUV, their faces partially obscured.

Rodney peered over his shoulder. "That was taken at the docks. Thought it was nothing at first, but now..."

Nicole felt a jolt of recognition as the details clicked into place. "The same SUV from the night of the fire," she said, her voice laced with urgency. "It has to be."

"They must have seen you taking pictures," James said, his expression grim.

"Bastards are more than just small-time crooks," Rodney muttered, shaking his head. "If they're tied to that, we've opened a real can of worms."

Nicole exchanged a glance with James, part fear and part determination. "Maybe that's why the woman called. Maybe she's with one of them."

"I've still got some connections in the law department; maybe I can get you some answers." Rodney said, packing his things quickly. "Then you'll know who you're dealing with."

Nicole nodded, grateful for his persistence. "Be careful," she urged as Rodney made his way to the door.

"Always am," he replied with a grin, though it didn't reach his eyes.

As the door closed behind him, James pulled Nicole into an embrace. She felt the solid weight of him against her, reassuring even when everything else felt precarious.

"You should call your dad back," James suggested, his voice gentle but firm. "Keep him in the loop."

Nicole hesitated, knowing how worried her parents would be. But James was right; they needed to be prepared, too.

She picked up her phone and dialed, her heart pounding as if it were a countdown.

Her father answered quickly, concern already evident in his voice. "Nicole? We've been worried sick."

"I'm okay," she said, trying to sound more certain than she felt.

"We heard about the fire," he continued, emotion tightening his words. "Why didn't you call us sooner?"

"I didn't want you to panic," Nicole replied, her voice softening. "It's been... complicated."

"You're coming here," he insisted. "We'll be there in an hour."

Nicole hesitated, glancing at James. His expression held understanding and something that looked like disappointment.

"I can't just leave right now," she explained, torn between wanting to reassure her family and seeing this through. "Not yet."

"Nicole—" her father started, but she cut him off gently.

"Please trust me. I'll come soon... I promise."

There was a pause on the line followed by a resigned sigh. "All right," he relented. "But call us if anything changes."

"I will." She hung up, feeling the weight of another promise added to the rest.

James rubbed his hand down her arm in silent support. "What did he say?"

"They want me to come home," Nicole said, sitting back down. "I don't know if I can handle them worrying like this."

"They care about you," James reminded her, his voice a mix of sympathy and something more.

Nicole nodded, knowing he was right but feeling the heaviness of it all pressing down on her. "I should have called them sooner."

James sat beside her, gathering the papers they'd spread out. "It's a lot to deal with. No one expected this."

She watched him for a moment, feeling a swell of gratitude for everything he'd done, everything he continued to be. Her mind drifted to the night on the porch, the way he'd looked at her—like none of this chaos mattered as long as they had each other.

"Thank you," she said suddenly, needing him to know how much it meant.

He looked up, surprised. "For what?"

"For being here. For..." She hesitated, the words hanging between them like an unspoken promise. "For everything."

James smiled, the kind that reached his eyes and made something inside her lift. "You don't have to thank me," he said, his voice low and sure.

But Nicole felt like she did; she needed to make it clear even in the middle of all this uncertainty. She leaned in and kissed him softly, a gentle affirmation of everything they hadn't yet said. It surprised both of them, its sweetness cutting through the worry like sunlight after rain.

He responded immediately, deepening the kiss with a tenderness that made her heart race. When they pulled apart, Nicole felt breathless but also more certain than she had in weeks.

"Wow," James said, sounding equally dazed and delighted. "I've been wanting to do that for a long time."

She laughed softly, a sound that was equal parts relief and newfound joy. "Me too."

They sat together in comfortable silence, knowing there was still so much to figure out but feeling like they'd crossed an important threshold. The tension between them had shifted, settling into something both frightening and exhilarating.

Eventually, the weight of the day grew heavy, and Nicole let her eyes drift shut on James's shoulder. She felt his fingers trace gentle patterns on her back; each touch a silent promise. She wanted to tell him everything right then—that she couldn't imagine facing any of this without him, that she was starting to believe they'd be okay—but exhaustion pulled her under before she could find the words.

She woke hours later, disoriented by dreams of fire and smoke. James was still beside her, his presence a calming constant. The room was dark except for a single lamp casting soft shadows across the walls.

"You're awake," he said quietly, brushing a loose strand of hair from her face.

"I didn't mean to fall asleep," Nicole replied, sitting up and rubbing her eyes. "How long was I out?"

"A while," James answered, smiling at her groggy, "—but you needed it."

Nicole stretched, feeling a hint of soreness from sleeping in the awkward position. "Sorry I left you hanging."

James shook his head, dismissing her apology. "It's nice seeing you relax a little."

But she couldn't fully relax, not with so many threads still unraveling around them. She stood, reaching for the stack of papers on the table. "We should keep working."

"We will," James said, rising to his feet and pulling her into an embrace. "But you need to take care of yourself, too."

His warmth was reassuring, but Nicole felt the anxiety creep back in as they returned to sorting through their notes.

The next few days passed in a tense blur. Rodney checked in occasionally with brief updates that left them wanting more—rumors of police corruption, mentions of bribes—but nothing concrete enough to act on.

Then one morning, just as Nicole was beginning to feel the weight of doubt settle heavily on her shoulders, her phone buzzed with a message from Rodney: "Got something big. Meet me at the diner."

She showed it to James, her eyes wide with hope and apprehension.

"This could be it," she said, feeling her pulse quicken.

"Let's go," he replied, grabbing his keys.

"No, I'll go.

"Are you sure,

"Yes, it'll only be for a while; besides, I need to clear my head and get some fresh air. She wanted to say she needed to get away from his tempting stare.

She left the house quickly, Nicole's mind racing with possibilities. The threat still hung over them, but his new lead was a flicker of light in an otherwise dark maze. She clung to it as they drove through town, her anxiety mounting with each passing block.

The diner was nearly empty when she arrived, its neon sign crackling against the morning sky. She spotted Rodney in a corner booth, hunched over a stack of papers and looking more disheveled than usual.

Nicole slid in across from him. "What did you find?"

Rodney leaned forward, his eyes sharp with urgency. "The captain has a mistress," he explained, more as a question than an answer.

She eyed him, both skeptical and intrigued, a mixture he'd seen too often lately. "Are you sure?"

He wished he could be. Rodney ran a hand through his prematurely gray hair, feeling the tension gather like a storm cloud. The silence around them suddenly seemed too loud, reminding him of what lay at stake.

Rodney read the message again, weighing each word. A typical bait, designed to be too alluring to dismiss: the captain has a mistress; she might talk. The kind of lead that could blow their investigation wide open or waste another day they couldn't spare. His gut, honed by years of digging, told him it was trouble. But they were short on other options, and the sense of chasing shadows was eating at him.

He tossed his phone onto the tabletop and watched it slide into a pile of neglected notes and theories. Rodney's life had become a mess of these lately, each piece a puzzle with no solution in sight. Nicole was right to be skeptical, but if this lead panned out, it might be their break.

He observed her looking back at him from the other side of the table, expertly ignoring both the waitress and the enticing breakfast menu.

Her face was set in that determined way he knew well, the one that meant she had something and wouldn't let go until she'd worn it down to truth or futility.

The diner was quiet. Rodney's voice repeated his findings until his gestures became more animated with Nicole's unresponsiveness.

"Is your hearing lost, or are you thinking about a certain fine-ass man?"

Silence. *Snap. Snap.* "Mrs. Winn...Mrs. Winn..."

She was shaken out of a deep daydream. "Yes." Her thoughts had been drifting to his eyes, his lips....

"Yes, you're thinking about a fine ass man, or yes, you have hearing loss. Are we finally ready for King Ding-a-ling?"

"Harassment, Rodney."

"It's not harassment if you like it."

"The captain has a mistress," she said, the words rushed but deliberate. "What does she have to do with—"

"Anything," Rodney finished for her, not bothering to hide his disappointment. "She sent us the photos. Down by the docks. Exactly what the picture captured. That's twice now, probably setting up his next job."

Her lips pressed into a thin line. "Figured you'd say that. But there's more." She hesitated, and he could see the frustration pinning her in place, a reluctance to let it go.

"Never isn't," he said. The irony wasn't lost on him.

She studied him for a beat, taking in his preoccupied glance at the phone. "You've got something else."

"My sources tell me she's not happy since he's deciding to cut her off financially after ten years of sleeping together," he admitted, tilting the phone so she could see the screen.

He watched her read, the skepticism deepening, then shifting. "My God, you'd think the wife would know."

"She does know; that's why he's cutting the mistress off. The wife lets him mess around so long as the money in the bank is rolling in. El Cap-ee-tan got a little too free with the extra income, and the wife told him to cut the mistress off or it's alimony time."

"So, you think the mistress will talk due to lack of funds?"

"I absolutely do. All is fair in money and love."

This could work. Wives were an unreliable source for journalists when their husbands's money was involved, especially if it affected their status in the upper echelon of society. A mistress, however, swung whichever way the money was going. And if it suddenly became unavailable to them, then maybe the captain's mistress would talk, for a price, of course.

"That's one hell of a source, Rodney."

"The gays know everything."

"The captain has a mistress?" she echoed, giving voice to the improbability of it.

"Yes," Rodney said. "And it's a possibility she'll speak about the captain."

"But what if?" She left it hanging, the same question mark that had driven them this far.

Rodney looked past her, seeing their entire operation playing out on corkboards and desktops around the room. The corruption was like a cancer, tangled and resistant. Every lead went cold or dirty. He'd never admit it to Nicole, but he was running on fumes.

"Even if it's a long shot," Nicole pressed, "we can't ignore it."

He knew she was right. It wouldn't be the first time the smallest tip led to something much bigger. Still, he needed her to know he wasn't buying in without reservations. "It's thin, Nicole. Anonymous."

"Then we verify," she said, her resolve as strong as ever. It was that certainty, more than the text, that finally tipped him over.

He grabbed the phone and nodded, mostly to himself. "Alright," he said, "let's see what else she knows."

The relief was palpable, a shift in the air between them. Nicole was already collecting her notes, throwing him that look of hers—equal parts gratitude and challenge—as they gathered themselves to leave.

He fell in step behind her, dodging the same intern and sidestepping the same heated arguments. Their work had made them unpopular lately, too many ripples in a pond people preferred still. As they hit the stairs, he paused to take one last glance at the chaos behind them. The mess wasn't just out there; it was in here, between them, pushing them further than they'd ever planned to go.

The late winter air hit like a wake-up call, sharp with the city's grit. "The captain's a careful man," Rodney said, watching her reaction.

"Then we make him careful enough to slip," she replied, not missing a beat. "Get dressed."

"Why do I need to be dressed?"

"You're coming with me."

"Alright. You're buying me dinner."

The stakes played out in his mind—a busted lead, another dead end. Or worse, a setup with real consequences. But underneath the doubt, beneath the worry, there was something else: the hope that this time, they'd get what they were after. As they headed toward the car, he let himself hold onto that. Just for a moment.

Trembling Truths

G uzman stood with his back to the window, contemplating the faint reflection of his own stillness in the glass. The room behind him hummed with urgency—a woman's defiant stare frozen in a surveillance shot, voices sparring with static on an intercepted call, Carlos's presence sprawling with cigarette smoke and confidence. Only the clock moved at its intended pace, but that too would be stopped. "She's had help from the start," Carlos said, as though breaking the news of a close friend's death. "We need to turn things up a notch."

The pictures were spread across Guzman's desk, each one more incriminating than the last. The woman should have been dead by now, her body discovered in an alley or floating by the docks. Instead, she haunted him with this paper trail of betrayal, still alive and still a threat. He picked up the top photo, the edges curled from where it had been gripped too many times, and studied it. Nicole Winn looked back at him with infuriating determination, her face clear even in the grainy shot.

"She won't get another chance," Guzman said, his voice a controlled whisper that cut through the air.

Carlos shifted in his chair, letting the smoke curl lazily from his lips. "You underestimate her, my friend. She's not alone in this." He gestured toward the photos with the tip of his cigarette. "Look how close they were last time. That's not luck."

The office bore witness to Guzman's power—a vast room that swallowed sounds and emitted none, with walls that exuded opulence through their understated elegance. Even the light seemed subservient, casting only the shadows he permitted. Guzman set the photo down, adjusting its angle as if placing a piece on a chessboard. "You think I'm not aware?" he asked, his tone suggesting that awareness was his currency and Carlos would do well to remember that.

Carlos shrugged, leaning back with an ease that defied the tension. "I'm saying this one might be out of your league," he said, with the unruffled demeanor of a man offering friendly advice over drinks rather than predicting the future to a crime boss.

The words hovered in the space between them, daring Guzman to react. But he remained silent, turning his gaze back to the desk, where a new collection of evidence awaited. Surveillance notes, phone records, and a digital thumb drive marked with the care of something that could explode at any moment. He sorted through them with methodical precision, his expression never changing but his intent sharpening with each second that passed.

"Too close this time," Guzman said finally, more to himself than to Carlos. He pushed the papers aside, revealing the glossy spread of images beneath. Faces caught in dark corners, meetings captured from impossible angles. It should have been enough to bury them. "If she has help, I want to know who."

Carlos nodded, the confidence never leaving his face. "We can do that. I'm telling you, she's had someone watching her back from day one. Professionals."

The suggestion of high-level interference didn't sit well, but Guzman's demeanor betrayed no concern. Instead, he looked at Carlos with a calculated calm. "Turn things up a notch," he said, echoing the words with new weight.

Now it was Carlos's turn to contemplate, his mind turning over the possibilities like a gambler assessing his odds. "We bring in someone," he said slowly, testing Guzman's reaction. "Out of town. No connections here. But good."

Guzman narrowed his eyes, a predator considering the value of its prey. "And this someone can get it done?"

"The CIA hires him when they want people gone. No traces," Carlos said. He flicked his ash onto the floor, ignoring the polished surface as he held Guzman's gaze. "Right now, you've got nothing but traces."

The silence in the room thickened, pressing in around them like the slow tightening of a noose. It was the only sound that dared persist. Guzman moved back to his desk, each step measured and deliberate, as though walking the distance to Nicole's funeral. He picked up another photo, this one showing Nicole beside a man—a man whose very presence added insult to the injury of her continued existence.

"Make the call," Guzman said, and there was nothing soft about his voice this time. It carried the weight of inevitability and the chill of an executioner's breath.

Carlos stood, slipping the cigarette pack into his pocket and leaving the spent butt on the desk. "Consider it done," he said, and the words held no more doubt than the bullet in a chamber.

Guzman waited for the door to close before sitting down, the room silent once more under his control. He looked at the photo of Nicole and the man—James Williams, whose reputation preceded him even here—and felt the anger that burned through his usual reserve. This was no longer a game of evasion. It was something much closer to home.

He set the photo down with the care of one tucking in a sleeping child, ensuring it stayed put until it was time to wake.

The authority of Guzman's command trailed behind Carlos like the echo of a gunshot. The brisk city air embraced him, free of the tension he'd left behind in the office. "Make the call." He smiled, savoring the aftertaste of power. The warmth of the cigarette traveled through him as he flipped open his phone, ready to reignite the same spark in their new out-of-town friend.

The line rang once, then went silent, as though even the network feared the man who answered. Carlos spoke casually, letting the city sounds mingle with his words. "I have a friend in town who's causing some trouble," he said. "Needs a special kind of fix."

He paused, waiting for the flicker of interest he knew would come. It arrived with the weight of an accomplice he'd used before—a subtle intake of breath, a silence waiting to be filled. "The job's local, but we need an outsider's touch. No connections. No traces."

There was another silence, but this one carried the promise of a sharpened blade. Carlos grinned, imagining the look on the man's face. "Thought you'd be interested," he said, relaxing against the wall as the cold crept into his bones. "We've got a reporter and an ex-operative in the mix. Real high stakes."

Carlos drew deeply on his cigarette, watching the smoke dissolve into the city air as he spoke. The casual confidence in his tone belied the deadly seriousness of the words. "She's been dodging us for too long, but this time we're not leaving anything to chance. You're our ace in the hole."

The voice on the other end was as efficient as Carlos remembered. "And the police?"

"We've got them covered. Corrupt and looking the other way. It's the woman we want dealt with." He relished the ease of their conversation, violence ordered like a drink at the bar.

"What's the timetable?" The question came with the weight of certainty, as though the hitman was already making arrangements to end her life.

Carlos liked how the question was asked—not if, but when. "A few days. Maybe less if you're up to it. The clock's ticking." He let the implication linger, knowing it would only sweeten the deal.

"Shouldn't be a problem." There was no hesitation, just the assurance of a man who'd pulled the trigger before.

Carlos nodded to himself, satisfied with the way things were unfolding. "Good. You'll be well compensated. This one is personal, so the boss is generous." The promise of payment was almost an afterthought; the hitman thrived on reputation and risk.

"I'll see you soon." With that, the call ended, leaving Carlos alone in the buzz of the street, already anticipating the next move.

He leaned against the building for a moment, letting the glow from his cigarette punctuate the chill of the late afternoon. There was a calm in knowing they'd stepped up their game. The sense of danger, of lives about to be shattered, wrapped around him like a favorite coat.

With the casual arrogance of a man whose hand had already been declared the winner, Carlos strolled back inside, carrying the promise of death in his pocket.

Guzman sat where Carlos had left him, unmoving and unflinching in the face of what was now a guarantee. The office was an altar of silence, every surface a reflection of his control. A print of James and Nicole occupied the center of the desk, demanding his full attention.

It wasn't merely the journalist who had become an obsession. Guzman saw Nicole as more than just a threat to be eliminated. She represented something much deeper—an affront to his power, a public defiance that demanded the swiftest of retributions. Every escape was another cut, and he did not take wounds lightly.

He let his gaze shift to the digital files, the 8x10s, and the web of surveillance images that had followed her like a predatory shadow. Guzman's plans never failed. But this time, even the plans had to be terminated, along with those who thwarted them.

Carlos's entrance broke the stillness, and Guzman glanced up, knowing the news before it was spoken. The satisfaction on Carlos's face was more than enough.

"He's on it. Says a few days."

Guzman returned to the photograph, his look colder than any words he might have used. The room seemed to hold its breath, waiting for his response, but he had none to give. The final word had already been spoken.

Carlos didn't need to hear it again. He left as quickly as he'd arrived, leaving Guzman to contemplate the faces that had, for a short time, thought themselves beyond his reach.

He studied the image, a patient predator with its paw raised above a nest of panicked mice. No chance to scatter, no chance to run.

Guzman set the photo aside with a slow, deliberate motion. This time, there would be nothing left alive to defy him.

Nicole eyed the lobby from across the boulevard, her pulse quickening with every passing second. It looked the same as it had the night before, when chaos ruled and nothing made sense. The Turf Hotel stood like a fortress, its neon sign flickering in the gray light of early morning. She felt vulnerable in the simple tracksuit and ball cap, but it was the price of staying unseen.

She caught sight of the SUV parked beside the entrance, a black beast with tinted windows glaring at her like an old enemy. Her heart thrummed with adrenaline as she started in that direction, pretending to be just another jogger in search of an empty street.

The closer she got, the more details emerged—the out-of-state plates, two men inside gathering their things. She pushed herself harder, legs pumping as she focused on getting close enough to catch the license.

Suddenly, a strong arm hooked around her waist, pulling her sharply into an alley out of sight. She barely registered what was happening before she was face-to-face with James, his expression a mix of relief and exasperation.

"Are you trying to get yourself killed?" he whispered, scanning the street behind him.

Nicole took a breath, steadying her voice. "You said they'd be gone by morning."

"They were supposed to be. I'm checking it out now." His eyes were sharp and calculating.

She pulled back slightly, fueled by frustration. "Why didn't you tell me? I'm not some amateur who needs babysitting."

James sighed, running a hand through his hair. "I didn't know for sure until last night. Rodney's on the cameras; we're keeping watch."

"While I what? Hide?" She shook her head, anger rising with her words.

"While you stay alive." His voice softened as he met her gaze. "I need you to trust me, Nicole."

"You can't be out here, looking the way you do."

"What do you mean this way?" Her defiance was met with a sudden intensity as James pulled her closer, capturing her lips in a kiss that stripped away all pretenses. She froze for a moment, then melted into it, her own guarded need rising to meet his. The danger around them only fueled the raw urgency, the certainty of everything else falling apart lending desperation to the one thing they were sure of.

Nicole broke away first, breathless and wide-eyed. The world had lurched and tilted around them, landing with a force she hadn't expected. "James—"

He cut her off, holding her steady. "I can't lose you," he said simply, the confession hanging between them like vapor in the chill air.

She wanted to speak, to insist that she could look after herself, but the words wouldn't come out right.

Instead, she nodded, feeling for once the full weight of what lay ahead. "Then we do this together," she managed.

For a moment, the city sounds faded into the background, and she remembered what it felt like to believe someone had her back. But the doubt crept in, fueled by secrets and unanswered questions. "I do," she said, though it felt like an unfinished thought.

James nodded, a trace of something almost like hurt flashing across his face. He released her arm but stayed close, vigilant. "I'll drive you to Renée and Noah. Get you somewhere safe."

Nicole hesitated. She'd promised herself she wouldn't run again, not unless there was no other choice. "We need those plates," she said, determination edging out fear.

"Rodney can get them the first second they move." James's voice was steady, reassuring.

Nicole bit her lip, knowing he was right but hating the helplessness of it. She felt caught between two fires—Guzman's men closing in and the distance growing between her and everyone she loved.

"Okay," she relented finally, feeling the weight of her decision settle over her like thick fog. "But I'm not waiting.

The sound of an engine roared to life, and they both turned as the SUV peeled away from the curb. Nicole watched it disappear into traffic, her heart a knot of anger and fear.

"Come on," James urged, pulling her deeper into the alley.

They reached a side street where his car was parked, and Nicole threw herself into the passenger seat, already dialing Rodney's number. "They're on the move," she said as soon as he picked up. "Black SUV, New Jersey plates. Did you get it?"

Rodney's voice was calm, steadying her panic. "I've got eyes on them. Hang tight."

She hung up and turned to James, who was already navigating the maze of streets with practiced ease. The morning rush had begun, cars clogging intersections and pedestrians spilling off sidewalks. It felt like they were wading through molasses, every second stretching painfully.

James kept glancing at her, his concern evident. "We'll catch up with them," he said.

The hitman carried his small suitcase up the steps of the hotel with the confidence of a man on a two-week cruise. Vacation, he thought, the name of this West Virginia place sounding exactly like one. He let the front desk clerk mistake him for a businessman with nothing but a briefcase of boring reports, then checked into his room overlooking the scenic mountains. Not his first choice, but perfect for the task.

The room smelled of cigarettes and something sour. He didn't mind; there'd be plenty of time for fresh air once this was over. He placed the suitcase on the bed, snapped it open, and began unloading its contents with the precision of a chef prepping his station. He smiled at the thought: an apron and toque instead of guns and silencers.

There was a knock on the door. So soon? He glanced at his watch, then peered through the peephole. It would be, he thought with amusement, just like Guzman to check in so quickly.

The room was small and basic, like all the best places. The kind where you paid cash and got breakfast that stuck to your ribs. He pulled out a bottle of whiskey, poured a generous glass, and waited for Carlos to let himself in.

When the phone beeped, he knew exactly what it would say. There was something comforting about efficiency—how it wrapped around you like a warm blanket, as inevitable and predictable as death itself.

Carlos walked in with the air of a man who owned the world but couldn't quite afford the upkeep. "How are the accommodations?" he asked, casting a disdainful look around the room.

"Nothing better than West Virginia," the hitman replied, unbothered by the lack of luxury. He took a sip of his drink, welcoming the burn as it traveled south.

Carlos pulled a chair up and sat backward, draping his arms over the backrest. "You get the message?" He couldn't mask the anticipation in his voice, the eagerness of a kid waiting for Christmas.

The hitman nodded. "Reporter and her boyfriend. One with a death wish, one with a death sentence. Got it covered."

Carlos lit a cigarette, exhaling a cloud of confidence. "You know who the boyfriend is?" he asked, intrigued by the lack of reaction from his companion.

"James Williams. He was on my side of the line a while back. A little payback, I guess." He downed the rest of his whiskey and poured another.

Carlos liked how casual the hitman was. It reminded him of the first time he'd been part of something like this, before the bodies had piled up and things had gotten messy. He flicked ash onto the floor. "You'll have some company. Guzman wants it fast, but he also wants it done right."

The hitman nodded. "Heard it before."

Carlos ignored the slight, treating it as if he were dealing with a temperamental artist. "Just saying," he continued, as if they were discussing the weather. "If you take care of it by tomorrow, there's extra in it for you."

The offer floated in the air like the smoke, and the hitman let it settle around him. "It's all extra, if you ask me. They'll be dead, whether it's tomorrow or next week."

Carlos grinned, though there was a hint of something else beneath it. Relief? Anxiety? Whatever it was, the hitman enjoyed seeing it. "Then Guzman's a happy man. Happy men pay better."

The phone rang, and Carlos jumped like he'd been caught in bed with the boss's wife. The hitman picked up on the first ring. "Yes?"

Guzman's voice carried the same cold weight it always did, like the last block of ice in a melting tundra. "Is Carlos there?"

The hitman handed the phone over, suppressing a smile. It was almost too easy, like shooting ducks in a barrel. Carlos grabbed it, reassuming his casual demeanor.

"Yes, boss," he said, trying not to sound as intimidated as he felt. "We're just going over details."

There was a pause, the silence filling the room like a gas leak. "Details," Guzman repeated, the word dripping with the poison of impending violence. "Make sure he understands the importance."

"He's got it," Carlos replied. He handed the phone back, but the hitman didn't bother with a goodbye. He set it down and waited for Carlos to finish squirming.

"Sounds like he's counting on you," Carlos said, standing up and brushing invisible dust from his sleeves.

"I get that a lot," the hitman replied, unruffled by the tension that had oozed into the room. "Text him when it's done."

Carlos nodded, the cigarette dangling from his mouth like an unfinished confession. "Good luck," he said, knowing the man wouldn't need it. Luck was for amateurs.

After the door closed, the hitman savored the silence. He glanced at the suitcase, at the contents carefully laid out, and felt the warm familiarity of the work to come.

He walked to the window, appreciating the vast view of the city before him, the stillness before the storm he would soon unleash. It was funny, really, how much people cared about little things like scenery.

When the work was done, and the news traveled like wildfire across the East Coast, maybe he'd take a few days to enjoy it.

Nicole surfaced from uneasy sleep, drawn to the surface by the insistent aroma of coffee. The soft lamplight in the bedroom pooled in comforting circles but left the corners to the dark. She felt James's absence like an imbalance on the Richter scale of her life, though it was only his side of the bed that was empty. For now.

She lay back, willing herself to enjoy the temporary peace, the mundane sound of a clock ticking as precious as a heartbeat. After a week of hushed plans and aborted escapes, the normalcy seemed unnatural, as though the world were mocking her vigilance. The smell of coffee wound its way back to her, enticing and familiar, urging her to enjoy small pleasures before they slipped away again.

Slipped away. Her thoughts moved back to Baltimore, where a file full of answers had dissolved into questions when the server vanished. And the old house where she'd hidden, believing she was close to Guzman's undoing. She knew the stakes, knew her chances, and even James's tactical reassurances couldn't drown out the inner voice that measured her time in shortened lengths. The room that had felt secure now loomed like an empty theater, full of exits but no audience to save the show.

Nicole breathed deeply and slid out of bed, wrapping the quilt around her shoulders against the chill of their situation. She followed the smell of coffee, its warmth drawing her toward the kitchen and the promise of James's presence. As long as they were here, in this house, she believed in the hope of that scent.

She found him leaning against the counter, the casual posture hiding a readiness she had learned to recognize. "You're up early," she said, accepting the mug he offered with a hand that felt steadier for the first time in days.

"Couldn't sleep," he replied, the edge in his voice acknowledging more than the pre-dawn hour.

"We're okay for now," she said, willing it to be true. "Aren't we?"

"We are," James said, but the look they exchanged did not have the clarity of coffee, rich and black, the way they both took it.

A distant sound caught her attention—an echo, almost a memory, of what the night before had brought. This time, though, it wasn't a hallucination. This time, the bullets were real.

"James!" she screamed, but he was already moving, knocking the table over and pulling her to the floor. She felt the heat of a bullet pass where she'd just been standing, the hiss of an object designed for her murder.

"Stay down," James ordered, covering her body with his. She obeyed, but her mind screamed in protest, refusing to believe that their sanctuary had been so easily breached.

He crawled to the window, peering out with the fluid movements of a man conditioned for situations like these. "They're in the house next door," he said. "They'll come over once they think we're dead."

"Who?" she managed to say, as if it wasn't obvious. As if she hadn't known this would happen.

"Men with guns," he replied. His words had the crisp efficiency of military maneuvers. "Guzman's men."

James pulled her by the hand, keeping low. She could feel his pulse in that brief contact, steady and strong, nothing like her own. "We need to move," he said, and she nodded, already out of breath though she hadn't even begun to run.

They crawled toward the basement door, ducking beneath the table and along the walls as more bullets struck. She thought of Noah, of Renee, of all the reasons she couldn't allow herself to die, and found new strength in the desperation. They reached the stairs and tumbled down them, a crash of adrenaline and panic.

In the basement, James went instantly to a panel in the wall. He opened it to reveal a small cache of equipment—gear she couldn't begin to understand. Tactical bags, night vision goggles, and enough weaponry to defend against an army.

"They're coming," Nicole said, the fear she'd held back breaking free at last. "James, they're coming."

His movements were calm and precise, the opposite of her fear. "We'll be gone before they get here," he assured her, strapping on a holster and tucking a gun into the waistband of his jeans.

Above them, they heard the front door crash open and voices shouting. The sound drove Nicole to a near-frenzy, but James remained focused, shoving equipment into a bag and slinging it over his shoulder.

"There's another way out," he said. "Follow me."

They crept to the far end of the basement, the floor above them shaking with the presence of intruders. Nicole felt as though her heart would tear itself to pieces, like paper ripping along the lines of her worst fears. She imagined each step the attackers took, each room they entered, knowing the basement would be next.

A small window sat high on the wall, leading out into the backyard. James knocked it open with a single motion and gestured for Nicole to go first.

She hesitated; the prospect of squeezing through a tiny window while bullets flew seemed as dangerous as waiting to be executed. But James was insistent, and she trusted him more than her own instincts right now.

"Go," he said. "I'm right behind you."

With shaking hands, she hoisted herself up, wriggling through the opening and falling awkwardly onto the grass outside. The damp chill was a slap to her face, and she almost laughed at the normalcy of the night.

They should have been dead by now. They should have been ghosts.

James was through the window a second later, his movements impossibly fluid for someone with his size and muscle. He helped her to her feet, and they sprinted across the yard to a waiting car. Nicole couldn't remember seeing it there, but nothing in her life was supposed to be there. Nothing made sense except the warmth of James's hand in hers, pulling her to safety one more time.

They threw themselves into the car, and James started it with a key she didn't know he'd had. The engine roared to life, shattering the night's silence like glass, like promises, like everything she'd thought was true about safety.

"What about them?" she asked, looking back toward the house.

"They'll keep searching," James said. "We'll be gone by the time they give up."

His confidence bolstered her own, but just barely. The adrenaline and fear took over as they sped down the gravel road, the house behind them an outline in the dark. They could see a single light in the basement window. It had taken her through the long night hours. It had guided her to morning. It was so much further away than it should have been.

They drove on, past empty fields and through the curtain of night, leaving behind everything that hadn't happened.

The hum of the engine lulled her to sleep, and by the time they'd arrived at the hotel, her nightmares were put to bed. James knew better than to think they'd last. He checked the room before heading in. Nicole went straight to the shower, a brief retreat from reality. James turned the phone over in his hands.

He tried Blake first. The line rang and rang, each tone a mark on the countdown clock they lived by. Guzman's men were closer now, gaining ground by the minute, maybe seconds. He pictured Blake sitting at his desk, surrounded by maps and screens, too busy coordinating diversions to answer. A comforting thought, if he let himself be comforted.

The call went to voicemail. James hung up and tried again, his determination mingling with impatience. "Come on," he muttered, envisioning the flood of intel that must be pouring in on Blake's end.

The hotel room felt larger than he remembered. Emptier. He kept the lights off, letting the cover of darkness shroud them from anyone who might be looking. There were too many people looking. Too many chances to slip, fall, and disappear.

The phone sat silent, mocking him. James listened for a response, knowing it wouldn't come, then closed his eyes. The absence of a ring echoed louder than a gunshot.

He slipped it back into his pocket and paced to the window, scanning the landscape. Trees. Water. Rocks. As far as he could see, as far as he couldn't. His mind worked through scenarios, each more precarious than the last. A sharp breath, then he moved on, unwilling to entertain failure.

The water stopped running, and he let out a breath he hadn't realized he was holding. His heart pumped faster, the rhythm of concern and love. He couldn't separate them anymore.

James paused at the bathroom door, listening. There was a soft sound—like music, like comfort, like her—and he wanted to stand there forever, let it fill him, then spill over into places he thought he'd locked tight.

The door opened, and Nicole stood there, wrapped in a towel. The corners of her mouth turned up, fighting against gravity and exhaustion.

"I thought you'd be halfway to Baltimore by now," she said, leaning into him.

"Without you? Not a chance," he replied. "You're the only one with the directions."

They sat on the bed, an island of warmth in an ocean of dark. He touched her shoulder, letting his fingers linger, reluctant to move but even more reluctant to let go.

"Shouldn't we be running?" she asked, but there was no urgency in her voice. Just an honest, bone-tired question that demanded an honest answer.

"Soon," James said, a promise wrapped in a lie.

She nodded, the strands of wet hair falling into her eyes, and he brushed them away with gentle precision. She closed her eyes and let him.

"Just need to catch my breath," Nicole murmured, but she was already too far under to know how little breath they had left.

James pulled the towel from her shoulders and joined her under the quilt. The events of the day spun around them, disjointed and incomplete. He imagined each frame of the story coming to a sudden stop, the threat freezing before it got too close, and he wondered how long they could keep their place before being edited out of existence.

Her body was warm, soft, and trembling. When he kissed her, she melted into him, and he felt the pulse of her survival dance against his skin. Alive. Safe. For the moment.

He wanted her to know him, to feel him, to see this truth through her disbelief. Her fingers were hesitant shadows, tracing the hard lines of his muscles, the contours of a man she had not dared to imagine. She closed her eyes and breathed him in, her heart thumping against his like a drumline. He pulled back, just a fraction, letting her explore, letting her be the one to close the distance. Her trust, like a newborn bird, is fragile and beautiful.

She returned to him, unguarded, her hands more insistent now, learning him in the dark. He stifled a groan, the sound of his restraint in her ear, and she paused, fingers hovering, searching his face for the danger she'd missed. But he opened his eyes, and she saw it: the depths of his wanting, the way it wrapped around her like a flame.

Her touch came back to him, tentative, then bolder, until he was the one to close the gap, his mouth on hers, sudden and fierce. He felt her surprise, the thrill of it, the way she answered him with equal urgency. Her disbelief shattered, falling away like broken glass.

He ravaged her face with his touch, then plunged his thumb into her core and his index finger into her most private place. Against her lips, he growled, "Don't you dare come until I say so." He traversed her body with a hungry mouth, settling where he craved her most. He positioned her over his face and his mouth, devouring her with a relentless rhythm as his fingers plunged into her over and over. She thought she might shatter from the intensity, her screams of ecstasy echoing through the rooms, muffled only slightly by the pillow she bit into. He was unyielding, and her pleasure was at his command.

Nicole woke briefly as her arm fell across his chest. She whispered his name like an incantation, as if the letters themselves could build walls against everything outside. He held her close, repeating it with a low, steady insistence that filled her dreams.

He watched her for a long time, not daring to blink, memorizing the shadows on her face and the angles of her body. If Guzman's men caught up, if the phone didn't ring, if all they had was now, he wanted to preserve it with every cell of his being.

When he felt her relax into deeper sleep, James slipped out of bed and stood in the hallway, torn between the need to keep her in sight and the need to keep her alive.

He moved quickly and quietly downstairs, avoiding the loose board that creaked and the carpet that whispered. His feet knew the way. He found the phone where he'd left it, next to the unopened bags and the boxes he hoped to unpack later. Much later.

If Blake wouldn't answer, he'd get someone who would. He dialed the number and waited. Once, twice, then the pickup. "Williams," the voice said.

"It's me," James replied. "We're in a tight spot."

"You've been in worse."

"Not sure about that."

Another pause. This one sounded like disappointment. "Want to tell me why I'm hearing about it now?"

"Couldn't call and chat, Dad. We were busy staying alive."

"That's supposed to make me feel better?"

"Guzman's after us."

"Hell, James, what kind of shit have you been stirring in? You know if you stir in shit, it's going to stink."

His father had always known how to take the side road instead of the highway, how to skirt the edges instead of coming straight on. It was a skill James had never admired. But now? He wondered if it was one he could learn in time.

"Got Nicole with me. The kid is with his other mom."

"Ah."

It wasn't much, but it was enough. His father understood more than most about families and obligations. He wouldn't say no.

"They found us once. I don't want to give them a second chance."

"Where are you?"

"Out of town."

"I gathered that, son."

James clenched his jaw, took a deep breath, and tried again. "Manassas, Virginia."

"That's a long way to drive just for a family reunion."

"Are you coming, or are you going to give me more grief?"

He heard the shift and knew that the old man was packing his bags even as they spoke. "Of course, not over the phone. I'd rather do it in person."

"That sounds about right."

He stared at the phone, holding the memory of the calls like photographs of a time they could still survive. Then he walked towards the bedroom where Nicole was still sleeping, still safe.

In the morning, they'd have backup even Guzman wouldn't expect.

Getting to Know You

A graying waitress set James's mug down with a soft clank, coffee steaming to the brim, before she slipped away, leaving him alone in the cracked vinyl booth. The early lunch crowd swirled around him—plates rattling, orders bellowed—yet no one spared him a glance, and he relished the anonymity. He kept his gaze low, every muscle coiled. He couldn't risk recognition—from old Baltimore associates who wouldn't hesitate to paint this place red.

The door jingled. Nicole's father slipped in, shoulders low with relief. He barely nodded at James before flicking his eyes over his right shoulder. James followed that look—and froze. His father stood in the aisle, fist half-clenched, eyes colder than the north wind.

They sat, neither speaking as James lifted the mug. He should've waited for it to cool, but he tipped it anyway. The scalding bitterness clawed at his throat, and each word that followed tasted of ash.

"Thanks for coming." He kept his voice flat, dangerous.

Nicole's father tapped the table. "Anything for Nicole."

James's father snorted. "What's going on?"

Before James could answer, Renée burst in, Rodney at her elbow. Her coat slapped open, breath misting in the air; her pulse hammered so loudly James could almost hear it. Rodney eased into the seat beside James, cracked leather notebook in one hand, the other fisting a Styrofoam cup like a lifeline. Renée slid in on James's other side, uncertainty and anger burning in her eyes.

"Start from the top," he said, voice strained. "She doesn't know half of it."

James's father leveled Rodney with a stare sharpened by suspicion. "Who are you?"

Rodney met it head-on. James noted the flicker in the old man's eyes—no recognition yet. "Rodney. Nicole's colleague."

Nicole's father shot James a look that could slice steel. "Why call us here?"

James braced both hands on the table. Steam curled from his ragged breath. "You know who I am. And yesterday they tried to kill Nicole—gunfire, close enough I saw the muzzle flash."

The two older men exchanged a loaded glance. James's father's jaw twitched; his knuckles whitened.

"And?" he demanded.

"I'm not running this alone. I need your help."

All fell silent but for the diner's hum and the hiss of the grill. Nicole's father leaned forward. "How do you know who's after her?"

James nodded at Rodney, who scribbled furiously. Then he spoke. "Our sources in Baldwin Gardens. They say it's the same crew."

"You think," James's father growled.

"They're connected. Deep." Rodney's voice rose, drawing curious glances. He leaned in, lowering it. "They've got hitmen here."

James's father leaned back, arms folding. "What do you want from us?"

"Your advice," James said, voice taut. "How to handle it so no one dies."

Nicole's father tapped his finger. "Heroism gets people killed. Are you sure you're not trying to play hero?"

"No one else needs to get hurt," James said softly.

"So, no hero," his father concluded.

Nicole's father closed his eyes a moment. "Isolate them. Cut off their backup. Don't let anyone else roll in."

Rodney flipped the notebook open again, poised to write. Renée leaned toward James. "How do we do that?"

James's father's tone shifted, respect creeping in like a tide. "We draw them in—somewhere we control. Trap them."

Rodney raised an eyebrow. "Ambitious."

The old man cracked the barest grin. "Got a better plan?"

Nicole's father pulled out his phone. "I'm calling for backup." He tapped and held the line. "Hey—got a minute?" A muffled reply came. "Yeah. It's fine. Hold on." He set it on speaker.

"Ok, shoot," said the grainy voice.

"Remember those fireworks we used to set off?" Nicole's father asked.

Recognition sparked between the two men. James's father nodded once, sharply.

"Got it," the speaker said. "Where?"

"Thirty minutes from Ocean City. No neighbors, no witnesses."

"Send your neighbors on vacation," the voice said. "When those guys show, light 'em up."

Renée froze. James caught her trembling. He met her eyes. "Dad's neighbors. You and Noah stay at the hotel down the road."

She bit back a retort, fear flashing behind her anger. Then she nodded, rigid. "Fine."

Nicole's father killed the call. "We'll reconvene soon."

James exhaled. "We'll nail down the details. Make sure no one tails us."

Rodney made a final note. "It's dangerous. But if it works—"

Nicole's father sighed. "You'll owe me."

James allowed a tight, almost predatory smile. "Not the first time."

They hashed out specifics for another hour, then rose, slipping out separately to shake any tails. James tossed his bags into the car; he knew his main goal was to get back to Nicole and give her the details.

He drove toward the hotel, glancing at the rearview every few seconds, turning his route into a maze. Finally sure he was in the clear, he parked and hauled his bags up the stairwell, each step echoing his urgency.

Nicole was in the room, seated on the edge of the bed, the TV flickering with news of another shooting. Her eyes locked onto his, the question already there.

"Got it all worked out," he said, breathless. He laid the plan out like a map, each piece fitting into place as he spoke. Her worry carved lines into her face.

"What if it doesn't work?" Her voice caught, a thread unraveling.

He moved to her, arms drawing her in. "It will," he murmured, feeling the tension in her body, the fragile belief.

She held him tighter, the phone ringing beside her, Renee's name flashing across the screen. She ignored it, burying her face against him. When she finally spoke, he heard the resolution there, like steel newly forged.

"We're in this together," she said, pulling back to look at him fully.

He nodded. "All the way."

James looked at Nicole, intensity burning in his eyes. He bent down slowly toward her lips; he didn't want to scare her away. She stayed perfectly still, and he kissed her, tasting each moment. The sound she made gave him the encouragement to delve in more.

Her fingers twisted in his hair as if anchoring him to this world. His mind stopped racing, the maze outside disappearing into the ether. He felt her heartbeat, thunderous against his own.

The kiss became more intense with each movement of his mouth. Their tongues danced against one another. She pushed closer, his hands finding the curve of her back, her breath warm against his skin. He felt the urgency in her, a longing that matched his own, entwining them tighter than any plan or promise.

"I want to taste more of you." James said.

He moved lower, kissing along her neck, feeling the thrum of her pulse as she whispered his name like a prayer. He was losing himself in her, the world outside receding into whispers and shadows.

"I need you." Her voice broke through, pulling him back to her eyes, deep and unguarded.

He ravaged her body with fierce kisses, descending hungrily towards her feet while tearing her underwear down.

"Against the wall. Now." His voice was a low growl.

She obeyed, her gaze locked onto his, her back pressed against the cold plaster. He dropped to his knees, his shoulders level with her knees, and hoisted her up, her legs straddling his shoulders. Bracing against the wall became her only anchor as his mouth unleashed a torrent of sensations she had never known. His lips devoured, suckled, and slurped, while his tongue lashed and swirled, driving her moans to cries of raw passion and screams of sheer ecstasy.

Sensing her orgasm teetering on the edge of explosion, he plunged his head lower, his tongue invading the intimate crevice between her clitoris and ass. She came undone, thrashing wildly, clutching his head with an insatiable urge to bury his face deeper into her core. Her pleasure became a savage, all-consuming force, shattering every fiber of her being.

She thought she was spent, but he wasn't finished with her.

With a deliberate, torturous slowness, he lowered her onto his body, his fingers insistently circling her clit, stoking the embers of her climax back into a roaring blaze. Her body convulsed, wild and uncontrollable, as he wrung every last drop of pleasure from her. When her shudders finally ebbed, his voice was a low, commanding growl. "Take off my pants. Slowly."

She obeyed, fingers trembling with anticipation. When he sprang free, he sat on the edge of the bed, gripping her hips to impale her on his length. She felt him fill her, stretch her, and complete her. A new sensation began to build, not like the focused intensity of before, but a consuming, all-encompassing heat. He guided her movements, teaching her how to take him, how to pleasure them both.

She gripped his shoulders, her pace increasing, her body writhing. Her hands were on his shoulders, her body splayed open. Her body was his to control. He pressed his finger to her ass, and her world shattered. A scream tore from her throat as an orgasm unlike any other ripped through her, the brutal, relentless waves leaving her shaking and gasping.

They fell back onto the bed, urgent and breathless, the threat beyond the walls a distant echo. His hand pressed against her, finding heat and softness, his own breath catching at the feel of her beneath him. She arched into him, a soft cry escaping her lips.

Time folded in on itself, and he was lost to the moment, to her.

Later, they lay tangled in sheets and each other, silence stretching around them like a held breath. She traced patterns on his chest, lines that felt like promises.

"Whatever happens," she said, her voice softer now, "I'm not letting you go."

The leather of Guzman's chair creaked under the weight of his barely contained rage. His men flinched at the violent, guttural sounds of the old man's Spanish curses, ricocheting off the cold concrete walls of the abandoned building. He told them they were useless. Incompetent. Little girls. They bowed their heads, only looking up when their boss's rage quieted to a few rasping breaths. Guzman stood abruptly, flinging a glass at the wall. It shattered, its crystalline carcass hitting the ground a moment after the door did. The men vanished like rats from a spotlight.

He seethed, pacing back and forth across the dingy office, his fine Italian shoes crushing the shards beneath them. She should have been dead already. His mistake had been leaving her to her own devices after her mother and father had gotten out of town. Now here she was, digging around, threatening his work, threatening everything. He could almost feel her breathing down his neck and hear her accusing words with every second that passed.

Guzman took a deep breath, steadying himself, trying to switch gears from wrath to calculation. She wasn't the kind of person you just killed outright—not without expecting hell to rain down afterward. Too much noise. Too many people are asking questions. That's why he'd left her alone. He thought she'd move on. But now she was here, right in his city, too close to his empire.

His phone rang, a sharp interruption of the thoughts swirling in his head. He pounced on it, barking into the receiver. "¿Dime?"

"It's me," came Carlos's voice, tinny and too calm. "Just wanted to let you know, our guy has been following them. He'll brief you in twenty minutes."

Guzman clenched his jaw, rolling the tension through his shoulders. He needed this done. Swift. Quiet. He needed to show the girl what happened to people who got too close. "Good," he said, his voice low and dangerous. "Make sure this one doesn't get away from you."

Carlos paused. "I don't know, boss. Maybe you should have just killed her sooner, before she—"

"¡Imbécil!" Guzman's hand tightened around the phone, turning his knuckles white. "Do I have to do everything myself?"

"No, no, no! Boss, we're on it. We won't let you down."

"If I hear about another screw-up, Carlos," Guzman said, the calm in his voice even more chilling than his anger had been, "I'll let you see how it feels when people don't follow orders. You hear me?"

Carlos swallowed audibly on the other end. "Got it, boss. Consider it done."

Guzman slammed the phone back onto the desk, his heartbeat a staccato in his ears. He wiped a bead of sweat from his brow, allowing himself the barest moment of relief. Then, with a sigh, he began to pace again.

The door opened cautiously, the tiniest crack, and one by one, his men crept back in. They hovered just inside the entrance, waiting, eyes cast down. Guzman watched them for a moment, taking pleasure in their obvious fear, letting them squirm before addressing them.

"Get your asses back to work," he growled. "That little girl isn't the only one of you who'll be dead if this man fails. Make sure he doesn't. Tell him who she is. You hear me?"

They nodded in unison, a flock of bobbing heads, and Guzman knew that their newfound zeal would ensure the hit man's success.

"Go!" he barked.

They scattered, leaving him alone in the dim room. He collapsed back into his chair, the leather protesting again under the weight of his anger. He closed his eyes, plotting revenge, wondering if Carlos's plan was good enough, and hating that the girl was now so close he had to even ask the question.

Shadows from the Past

Nicole's hands gripped the steering wheel, steady despite the ache in her muscles. The trees loomed like sentinels along the gravel road, their branches interlocking overhead in a whispered conspiracy. She hadn't passed a single car since she'd turned off the main highway. The solitude was comforting, but she knew better than to let her guard down.

Her father's directions had been precise, and when the road broke into a clearing, the cabin stood waiting, its silhouette softened by the early evening light. She parked the car and sat for a moment, the engine ticking as it cooled, the weight of the drive settling into her bones. The lake was a dark sheet behind the cabin, a boat moored to its dock.

Inside, the cabin smelled of cedar and dust, a relic of summers past. Each step creaked beneath her as she moved from room to room, opening closets and drawers with a deliberate calm. She found a hunting knife in the kitchen and a fishing rod in the corner of the living room, relics of her father's restless hands. A coil of unease curled inside her, but she shrugged it off and brought her bags in from the car.

The first night, she didn't sleep well. Dreams darted in and out, a flicker of shadows and soft voices that seemed to linger in the corners of the room when she woke. She rose with the sun and sat on the porch with a cup of coffee, watching the mist lift from the water. The air tasted of pine and possibility, and she resolved to spend the day unpacking the boxes she'd brought from the city.

By afternoon, the cabin felt more like her own. Books lined the shelves, and her clothes hung in the bedroom closet. She took the boat out to the middle of the lake, the rhythmic pull of the oars soothing her mind. There, bobbing on the water, she felt the thinness of the distance between herself and the thoughts she'd left behind. But when Renee's car pulled into the clearing, she realized the distance wasn't thin enough.

Renée stepped out with a grin that was both familiar and new, like a song Nicole hadn't heard in years. "Surprise!" she called, her voice echoing off the trees.

Nicole pulled the boat to shore, the awkwardness of her movements betraying her unease.

"I thought you might want company," Renée said when Nicole reached the dock, wrapping her in a hug that smelled of lavender and city air.

Nicole laughed, a brittle sound. "How did you find me?"

"Your dad," Renée replied, then pulled back, searching Nicole's face. "Aren't you glad I'm here?"

"I am," Nicole said, and she was, though not in the way Renée needed her to be. She watched as Renée unpacked wine and cheese from a tote bag, the ease of her gestures a counterpoint to the

heaviness in Nicole's chest. They sat on the porch, the sun dipping low, the wine loosening Renée's chatter. Nicole listened, letting Renee's voice settle over her like a warm blanket she wasn't sure she wanted.

"Remember that summer we drank tequila in the park?" Renée said, her eyes bright with nostalgia. "We thought we were such rebels."

Nicole nodded, the memory surfacing with a bittersweet clarity. She'd felt invincible then, like the future was a horizon she could shape with her own hands. "We were," she said, half-smiling.

Renée leaned back, looking out at the lake. "This place is amazing. So different from our home."

"It's a change," Nicole agreed, feeling again the tug of the distance she'd come here to create. "It'll keep me safe for now."

"But not forever, right?" Renée asked, a hint of something—curiosity, concern—edging her voice.

Nicole took a sip of wine, feeling its warmth spread through her. "Can we not do this now?"

Renée's eyes narrowed slightly. "What? Talk about what's happening with us?"

"Nothing is happening," Nicole said, the words too quick, too thin.

"James is happening," Renée countered, her voice sharpening. "Ever since the fire, ever since we moved into his house, it's like you don't see me anymore."

Nicole felt the knot in her chest tighten. "I don't want to argue."

"Then stop avoiding," Renée shot back. "We haven't touched each other in months. Not since we moved in with him."

"That's not true."

"Isn't it?" Renée stood, the suddenness of her movement startling. "Are you sleeping with him?"

Nicole flinched at the accusation, though she'd long feared it would come. "Renée, come on. You know it's not like that."

"I don't know anything anymore," Renée said, arms folded like a shield. "You left without even saying goodbye."

"Because you wouldn't have let me go," Nicole murmured, her voice tangled with guilt.

Renée turned away, the silence between them thick and crackling. "I can't believe you didn't even tell me you were leaving town," she said, softer now, the hurt like a raw nerve. "I had to hear it from your dad."

Nicole reached for her, but Renée didn't turn. Instead, she walked to the edge of the porch, her silhouette stark against the rising moon.

She leaned against the porch rail, her back to Nicole. "I thought maybe you'd want to figure things out together. But I guess you need to do it on your own."

"That's not what I want," Nicole said, each word a careful step on thin ice.

"Then what do you want?"

Nicole hesitated, the answer a fragile thing she wasn't ready to give. "Time. Space."

Renée let out a bitter laugh. "Right." She turned, meeting Nicole's eyes. "You need to decide, Nic. Which life you want. Because I'm not going to hang around and watch you disappear."

The porch light cast shadows on her face, softening the hard edges of her expression. "Renée," Nicole started, the word a plea.

"I'm serious," Renée interrupted, her voice steady. "You, me, or James. Just let me know."

Nicole watched, helpless, as Renée gathered her things. The tote bag banged against her leg as she walked to the car. Nicole sat rooted, each step Renée took pulling something from her. She half-expected Renée to pause, to look back, but the car door slammed with a finality that echoed through the clearing.

The engine started, headlights cutting across the darkening trees. Then Renée was gone, leaving Nicole alone with the hum of cicadas and the chill of the evening air. She stayed on the porch long after the taillights disappeared, the silence heavy with what hadn't been said.

Inside, the cabin felt larger and emptier, the shadows deeper. She poured another glass of wine and stared at it, as if it might hold an answer. The old clock in the living room ticked its slow rhythm, and she found herself counting the seconds, the minutes, the space that was already growing between them.

When she finally went to bed, the moon was high, and the sheets felt cold against her skin. The dreams returned, and she woke up with Renée's voice tangled in her mind. I need some time, she'd said. Time. As if it were a thing they could stretch or shorten at will. As if it wouldn't undo them. Nicole lay staring at the ceiling, thinking of Renée's smile, the way it used to chase shadows from a room, and she tried to picture life with Renée on her own terms. A life where they both had their space. A life that maybe didn't include James.

But James kept coming back. In thoughts. In dreams. In the way her body reacted when she imagined his hands, his lips. She closed her eyes, remembering the urgency of their last kiss, how it left her unsteady, breathless. She hated herself for wanting him now, for wanting anything other than Renée and the life they'd planned. But there it was, gnawing at her like a hunger she couldn't satisfy.

A sharp knock at the door startled her. She wasn't ready for another fight. "Renée, I told you I just need time. I don't want to—"

She opened the door, and it was James. Before she could react, he pulled her to him, his mouth on hers with a force that left her unbalanced. She kissed him back, a fierceness in her that startled her into wanting more.

They stumbled inside, a tangle of limbs and urgent need. She felt the rough press of the wall against her back, the heat of his body, and she let herself be lost in it, in him. Her breath came in gasps between his kisses, and she pushed him away just enough to see his face, to know she wasn't dreaming again.

"How do you know what I need?" she breathed, half-dazed, half-wondering.

He laughed, low and breathless, his forehead against hers. "I have my ways." His hands framed her face, drawing her back into their orbit.

She should stop. She shouldn't have let this happen. But when he kissed her again, everything she'd held tight unraveled, and she gave in to it, to him, completely.

After, they lay tangled on the floor, the night settling into his breathing, her breathing, the rhythm of their hearts.

"You left in the middle of the night," James said, a teasing reproach in his voice. "I woke up and you were gone. Not even a note."

The words lodged like a stone of guilt in her throat. "I thought it would be easier than a long, drawn-out goodbye."

"Easier for who?"

She ran her fingers through his hair, the softness of it, the nearness of him, more than she'd let herself hope for. "I didn't think you'd understand."

"Try me," he said, pulling her closer.

She hesitated, then let the truth slip out before she could stop herself. "I'm not sure I can do this," she confessed, her voice brittle with doubt.

He shifted, propping himself up on one elbow, searching her face with an intensity that made her chest tighten. "Do what?"

She looked away, the corners of the room blurry with the weight of her thoughts. "Any of it. You. Renée. Trying to be everything for everyone."

"Hey," he said, gently turning her face back to meet his gaze. "What do you want, Nicole?"

"I don't know," she said, the admission like a crack in the armor she'd built around herself.

He smiled, a slow, patient smile. "That's a start." He kissed her forehead and stood, pulling her to her feet. "Come on. Let's go outside."

The air was crisp against her skin, the lake a dark mirror beneath the moonlight. Nicole watched James settle on the porch steps, so sure of himself, so sure of her, and felt the pull of everything she was trying to escape. She sat beside him, the chill of the wood seeping through her clothes.

"Don't hide from me," he said, his words more request than demand.

She hugged her knees to her chest, her eyes on the water, thinking of the phone call from Renée, the shock of it still reverberating through her. Couldn't you at least tell me you're leaving town? The way her voice cracked open. She hadn't meant to hurt her. She hadn't meant to hurt anyone.

"What if I can't choose?" she said, her voice a thin thread.

James wrapped his arm around her, his warmth a brief shelter. "Then don't," he said simply.

She let her head fall against his shoulder, the ease of his answer almost unbearable. They sat like that for a long time, the night folding in around them.

When she woke in the morning, James was gone, and at first, she thought she'd dreamed it all. But the indentation of his body next to hers was real, and so was the note on the table, scratched in his quick, messy handwriting.

Gone for coffee.

She crumpled it in her hand, feeling the sharp edges of her uncertainty.

The day was overcast, the lake dull and uninviting. She rowed out anyway, her muscles protesting the effort. The air was heavy, pressing down on her. She let the oars rest and drifted, the emptiness of the landscape matching the emptiness inside her.

When she returned to the cabin, she poured herself a drink and stood looking out the window, watching the sky darken with the threat of rain. The sound of the phone ringing cut through the silence, startling her. She let it ring, each insistence a pull she resisted.

The answering machine clicked on, Renée's voice filling the room. "I'm heading back to pick up Noah from school. I just wanted to make sure you're okay." There was a pause, a moment of held breath. "I'm not sure if you got my last message, but I booked another night in town in case you change your mind. I'll be here."

Nicole closed her eyes, the drink bitter in her mouth. She imagined Renée at the motel, the clean lines of the room, the uncertainty in her hands as she unpacked the essentials she always carried. She imagined the way Renée would sit on the edge of the bed, expectant, hopeful, waiting for a knock or a phone call that might not come.

Placing her glass down, she ran her fingers over the note James had left, its edges softening where she'd crumpled it. Her eyes moved from the note to the phone, and she felt the weight of her indecision like an anchor.

Renée pulled into the school parking lot, her fingers tapping an anxious rhythm on the steering wheel. The day had been long and restless, the motel room a place of waiting she couldn't stand. She'd left Nicole four messages, each one more vulnerable, each one more of a risk. She told herself she'd only stay if she heard back, but she didn't believe it.

The playground was empty, kids long gone except for a straggler being led across the lot by a tall man with a baseball cap pulled low. Renée squinted, recognizing the bright orange of Noah's backpack. She slammed the car into park.

"Noah!" she called, her voice carrying through the cool afternoon air.

The man stopped, turning slowly, and Renée felt the first cold prickle of fear. Noah stood beside him, wide-eyed and frozen. The man's hand moved to his waistband, and Renée saw the glint of a gun.

"Don't make a sound," he said, his voice calm, steady. He crouched, his face level with Noah's. "Stay quiet and you'll be okay. Understand?"

Noah nodded, his eyes round with fear.

Renée's heart hammered in her chest. She forced herself to breathe, to think past the panic. "What do you want?" she asked, keeping her voice as steady as she could.

The man's gaze shifted to her, calculating. "You're gonna drive us out of here," he said, as if it were the simplest thing in the world. "And you're not gonna do anything stupid."

She nodded, desperation clawing at her insides. "Just let him go," she pleaded. "He's only a kid."

The man smiled, a quick, unsettling flash of teeth. "Then you better do exactly what I say."

He walked them to the car, his hand a firm grip on Noah's shoulder. Renée got behind the wheel, her hands shaking.

"Where are we going?" she asked, trying to keep the tremor out of her voice.

"Just drive," he said, sliding into the backseat with Noah.

She pulled out of the lot, her eyes meeting Noah's in the rearview mirror. He looked so small, so impossibly brave. She wished she could promise him it would be okay, that she'd get them out of this. But the man's presence was a dark weight, pressing down on her.

"Take the main road out of town," he instructed, the gun resting in his lap, a silent threat.

She drove, her mind racing, trying to replay everything Nicole had said about her father's cabin, its exact location. The road stretched out before them, empty and endless, the trees a blur of green and brown.

The man leaned back, his posture relaxed, as if he'd done this a hundred times. "How far's the cabin?" he asked, his tone almost conversational.

"About an hour," Renée replied, her voice tight.

"Good," the man said. He looked at Noah. "You doing okay, buddy?"

Noah didn't answer. He kept his eyes on Renée, searching her face for reassurance she couldn't give. She felt sick with the effort of keeping herself composed. She had to think, to act. But every plan seemed to dissolve under the weight of the man's presence, the finality of his gun.

"Make a left up here," he said, pointing to a narrow road with a convenience store at its entrance.

"Stop and put the car in park."

She turned and stopped the car, the gravel crunching under the tires. They were getting close, the cabin a destination that loomed with each mile they covered.

"Why are you doing this?" she asked, her knuckles white against the wheel.

The man laughed, a low sound that curled around them. "It's just business."

Renée felt a thin thread of hope. If it was about money, maybe he'd take it and leave.

"Both of you, out," the man said, tucking the gun into his waistband.

They went into the store, the harsh fluorescent lights making everything feel sharper, more dangerous. The man picked up a juice for Noah, not realizing James was parked two rows behind, watching in horror.

James sat frozen, a low curse escaping his lips. He'd been on his way back to the cabin with breakfast, Nicole's favorite pastries in a bag beside him. He hadn't expected to see Renée's car this far out, and now, with the man and the gun, it all clicked with a terrifying clarity.

He grabbed his phone, his mind racing. He could confront the man now, but he'd be risking Noah. He'd be risking Renée. He had to think. He had to be smart. He dialed his father, his fingers clumsy with urgency.

"Dad," he said when the line picked up. "You and Mr. Winn get ready. He's here, but he's got Renée and Noah. Stick to the plan."

He watched from his rearview mirror as the man walked Renée and Noah back to the car. A sick fear settled in his stomach, but he willed himself to stay calm, to stay smart. As soon as they pulled out onto the road, he started the engine and drove, the tires screeching against the asphalt.

He reached the cabin in minutes, the car a blur past the trees. Nicole was on the porch, her face unreadable as he ran up, breathless with panic and urgency.

She opened her mouth to speak, but he cut her off, the words tumbling out. "Renée," he said, the name like a trigger. "The man's got her. And Noah."

Her eyes widened, and she felt the shock of it ripple through her.

"Where?" she asked, her voice tight with fear.

"On their way here. We have to be ready."

She nodded, the color drained from her face but her resolve hardening. They gathered everything they could, moving with a frantic precision that left her breathless.

Nicole wished she'd kept the gun, but she knew they had backup. They just needed to hold out until

James' father showed. She forced herself to stay calm, to think in steps, to trust.

James watched the road, his face tense, every muscle in his body coiled. "There," he said, pointing to Renée's car as it pulled into the clearing.

"Stay back," Nicole urged, her voice shaking with a mix of terror and determination. "Let me try first."

He hesitated but nodded, retreating inside, out of sight. She took a deep breath and stepped forward, the gravel shifting beneath her feet.

The man got out, keeping a firm grip on Noah, his eyes sweeping the area with a predator's awareness. Renée followed, her face pale, her steps unsteady. "Nicole," she called, her voice cracking with both relief and fear. "He's got a gun."

Nicole felt the air shift, the clearing suddenly alive with possibility. Two shots rang out, their sound sharp and commanding. The man froze, his eyes narrowing as he scanned the trees, the first trace of uncertainty flickering across his face.

Renée's breath caught, and she took the moment to pull Noah closer, wrapping her arms around him. She could feel him trembling against her, and she whispered a promise she hoped she could keep. "It's going to be okay."

The man cursed under his breath, his control slipping but not gone. He tightened his grip on Noah's shoulder, the gun now a visible threat. "Who else is here?" he shouted, his voice losing its calm.

Nicole stepped forward, her heart pounding. "It's over," she said, her voice steadier than she felt. "Just let them go."

The man's eyes darted, calculating his next move. "Come on out Williams." he taunted, pulling Noah tighter.

Renée caught Nicole's eye, a flicker of fierce determination passing between them. She pushed the man with all her strength. "Run!" she screamed at Noah.

Nicole lunged forward, grabbing Renée's hand, pulling her towards the cabin.

The man cursed, the gun pulled from his waistband. Noah stumbled, but James was there, grabbing him and sprinting for cover. Another shot cracked through the air, hitting the gravel near their feet.

"Keep going!" James yelled, shoving Noah ahead and turning back for Renée and Nicole.

The man was closing in; his face twisted with rage. Nicole felt Renée's hand slip from hers as she pushed her forward. "Go!" Nicole shouted, the word a plea, a command.

Renée hesitated, torn between fear and the impossibility of leaving Nicole behind. But James was there, pulling her to safety, his grip a promise.

Nicole ran towards the trees, the man's footsteps heavy behind her. She willed herself not to look back, not to falter. Her breath was ragged in her throat, each step an eternity.

A shot echoed, splintering the air. She cried out, a sharp pain radiating through her leg as she fell. The ground was cold and unforgiving, the trees a blur above her.

She gritted her teeth and forced herself up, stumbling towards the water. Behind her, the man was closing in, his breath hot on her trail. She crossed an open patch of ground, the dock suddenly in sight, a tethered boat their only hope.

"Renée!" Nicole's voice cut through the panic, and she saw them—Renée, James, Noah—waiting at the water's edge, their eyes wide with terror as she neared.

She pushed on, each step a battle. She reached them just as the man broke through the trees, the gun raised, a feral determination in his eyes. There was nowhere left to run.

Just then, two shots cracked from the lake, slicing the air. The man jerked back, a red stain blooming on his chest. Time seemed to slow, his mouth forming a silent scream, then another shot rang out, and he crumpled, lifeless on the dock.

"Got him!" The triumphant shout carried across the water, and Nicole looked to see James' father and her father on the boat, their rifles trained on the dock. Her legs buckled beneath her, relief and pain overwhelming.

Renée was there in an instant, her arms around Nicole, pulling her close. Her breath came in frantic gasps, and Nicole felt the warmth of tears against her neck. "You're okay," Renée whispered, the words breaking with emotion. "You're okay."

Nicole clung to her, exhaustion and pain blurring the edges of everything. "I didn't want to hurt you," she said, her words thick with emotion.

"Shh." Renée held her tighter, her own tears falling. "We'll figure it out."

James knelt beside them, his face a map of worry. "Nic," he said, brushing the hair from her eyes. "You're bleeding."

The world tilted, dimmed at the edges, and she managed a small, crooked smile. "I noticed," she said, her voice faint, distant. Then the dark folded in, and she heard Renée's voice one last time before everything went silent.

When she woke, the cabin was filled with the low murmur of voices and the comforting smell of coffee. Her leg throbbed, bandaged and propped up on a stack of pillows. James sat beside her, his hand gentle on her shoulder.

"Hey," he said softly, relief flooding his expression. "She's awake."

Renée appeared, her face drawn but hopeful. "Nic," she breathed, sinking down next to her. "You scared the hell out of me."

Nicole blinked, the memory of the dock and the gunshot flooding back with a vividness that made her chest constrict. "Noah?" she asked, panic creeping into her voice.

"He's fine," Renée assured her quickly. "He's fine. He's outside with his grandads."

Nicole nodded, the tension in her slowly unwinding. "And the gunman," she said, her voice still edged with the fear of it.

"Dead," James answered, his tone flat.

She let out a long, shaky breath, the reality of it settling in. "Was he one of the gunmen at the house that day?"

James shook his head. "He was hired by Guzman to kill you. I found this in his coat pocket."

He handed her a yellow manila envelope. Inside was a single piece of paper with the words "Winn. Nicole. $50,000" scrawled across it.

"We were so close to losing you," Renée said, her hand finding Nicole's.

Nicole looked from Renée to James, the enormity of it all pressing down on her. "I don't know what to say," she said, her voice small.

James squeezed her hand. "Just say you're okay."

Nicole nodded, trying to hold back the flood of emotion. "I'm okay," she said, though she wasn't sure it was true.

Tying Up Loose Ends

They reached the house at dusk, the suburban lights barely illuminating the silence between them. James scanned the hallway, his hand hovering near his waistband. Nicole fumbled with her keys, her mind swirling with unfinished thoughts from their conversation on the drive back. Renée watched them both, feeling like she was caught in a storm of secrets.

When they opened the door, Nicole gasped. There, seated casually on the couch, was Guzman, flipping through a stack of photographs that spilled from a manila envelope. His presence was as commanding as it was unexpected.

James's reaction was instant; he drew his gun with military precision, eyes locked on Guzman. Nicole stood frozen in shock, confronted by the very subject of her years of investigation now materialized in her living room. Renée's face betrayed confusion mixed with an intuitive fear—how had he gotten in? What did this mean for them?

Guzman glanced up, unconcerned by the tension crackling through the air. "Is this how you welcome all your guests, James?" His voice was smooth, barely masking the threat beneath it. He placed the photos back into the envelope with a deliberate calmness that only made him more menacing.

Nicole found her voice, though it wavered slightly. "You're making a mistake coming here."

Guzman chuckled, an unsettling sound that reverberated in the charged silence. "I don't believe this is a mistake at all. It's time we had a conversation, no?"

Renée moved closer to Nicole, her eyes flickering between her and James, searching for answers in their tense expressions. "What is this? Who is he?" she whispered urgently.

James kept his gun trained on Guzman, but there was an edge of uncertainty now—as if he were calculating variables, options, and risks. "You have five seconds to explain what you want," he said, his voice steady.

Guzman leaned back into the couch, exuding an infuriatingly casual confidence. "Five seconds? I'm hurt, James. We go way back, after all." He gestured to the photos. "I think you'll find I have a lot of interesting things to talk about."

Nicole's heart pounded as she tried to organize the chaos in her mind. Years of whispers, threats, and near misses with Guzman's operations had led to this moment. She placed a hand on Renée's arm, both to reassure and steady herself.

James didn't lower his gun. "How did you find us?"

Guzman smirked, his eyes gleaming with a predatory satisfaction. "You're not the only one with friends in high places. Now, why don't we all sit down and discuss how we're going to solve this little... predicament?"

"And what predicament do you think that is?" James questioned, though a flicker of recognition in his eyes suggested he might already know.

Guzman smiled, a predator playing with prey. "The same thing you've always wanted—an agreement."

Renée tightened her grip on Nicole's arm, her fear now mingled with anger. She felt the weight of revelations still cloaked in mystery pressing down on her family. "This is about your investigation," she said, the accusation sharp.

Nicole swallowed hard, her mind racing to piece together a strategy. She turned to Renée, her expression a mix of apology and urgency. "He's part of the organization I've been tracking. The one that's been trying to stop me from publishing the article."

Guzman's amusement deepened. "You make it sound like we haven't already succeeded." He gestured around the room, his presence asserting control over their supposed sanctuary.

Nicole's eyes darted to James, seeking confirmation or denial of what Guzman implied. But James's face was inscrutable, a mask of professional detachment that gave nothing away.

"You're not untouchable, Guzman," Nicole countered, summoning her resolve. "I have enough evidence now to bring you down and everyone working for you."

He leaned forward, eyes narrowing with a dangerous gleam. "And yet here I am, sitting comfortably in your living room."

The truth of it struck her hard—Guzman's brazenness meant he knew something she didn't. That he wasn't afraid of what she had.

Renée watched the exchange unfold with growing clarity and dread. Pieces fell into place—the late nights, the evasiveness, the tension that had been tightening like a noose. Her voice was firm, demanding answers. "Nicole, how much danger have you put us in?"

Guzman answered before Nicole could, his tone laced with mock sympathy. "Oh, Nicole hasn't even begun to tell you the half of it. She's quite the risk-taker."

James's gun remained unwavering, but Nicole saw the flicker of conflict in his eyes—a connection to Guzman that was both advantage and liability. "I should shoot you now," he said, though they both knew it was more complicated than that.

"But you won't," Guzman replied smoothly. "Not when I can give you both what you want."

"What is it you think we want?" Nicole fired back, her voice edged with defiance.

"Proof," Guzman replied simply, waving the envelope like a baited lure. "You're not the only one with secrets to trade."

The room pulsed with a tense stalemate, every second stretching the constant moving. Her voice was brittle but fierce. "What else aren't you telling us?"

Guzman paused, assessing her with an unsettling amusement. He turned his gaze to Nicole, delivering his words with surgical precision. "Have you ever wondered, Nicole, how James came into your life so... conveniently?"

Nicole's stomach clenched. "What are you saying?"

James's grip on the gun tightened, but he said nothing.

Guzman's smile was cruel. "He knew exactly who she was all along. Convenient, don't you think, that the sperm bank made such an unfortunate mistake?"

Nicole's face drained of color as the implication hit her. "You switched the samples?" she whispered, horrified.

James lowered his gun slightly, his stoic mask cracking under the weight of exposure. "He was going to use his sperm to get revenge on you for writing those articles; I had to do something," he said hoarsely.

Renée reeled back as if struck, her world disintegrating around her. "So we were just part of your plan?"

Guzman savored every reaction with a sadistic pleasure. "Oh, the man actually cares," he taunted. "Isn't love grand?"

Nicole struggled to absorb the betrayal and its magnitude. Years of trust unraveled in an instant, leaving raw disbelief in its place. "All this time...?" she said, her voice breaking.

James's expression was tormented, words tumbling out in a desperate explanation. "I didn't know it would turn into this. I love you, Nicole. I thought I could protect you."

Guzman laughed, a sinister echo in the charged room. "And yet here you all are—exactly where I want you."

Renée felt anger rising through her shock like lava. The truths that had been kept from her now demanded release, more explosive than she ever imagined. She glared at James, her trust shattered. "You lied to us from the start."

Nicole staggered back, Renée's grip slipping from her arm. Her mind was a riot of betrayal and disbelief.

She struggled to comprehend the enormity of what had just been revealed. That the man she trusted had orchestrated his way into their lives through deception so profound it left her breathless.

"How could you?" Nicole's accusation cut through the tension, sharp with pain.

Nicole's heart ached, torn between anger and understanding as she met Renée's eyes. "I didn't know," she insisted.

James stood there, exposed but defiant. "To protect you," he answered, desperation edging his voice. "To keep you safe from him."

Nicole's thoughts spiraled; memories reassembled in brutal clarity. The way James always seemed to anticipate danger, his relentless vigilance—it all made sense now, twisted sense. They'd been living side by side with a truth built on lies.

Guzman watched them with the satisfaction of a master puppeteer whose strings were perfectly taut. "This is what happens when you try to play my game," he said, savoring the chaos.

Nicole's vision blurred with emotion, the room around her closing in. All the while, James had been maneuvering them through a labyrinth she never even knew they were in. Her betrayal cut deep—a wound layered with love and anger.

Renée's voice was tightly controlled, though her eyes burned. "We can't trust anything you've ever said."

"I know," James replied, agony seeping into his words. "But you can trust that I—"

"You think this is about trust?" Nicole interrupted, her voice rising. "You manipulated our entire lives!"

Guzman rose from the couch, his presence commanding. "Now that we're all caught up on the family drama, how about we talk business?"

James and Nicole exchanged a look—wariness mixed with reluctant understanding that this wasn't over yet.

She turned back to Guzman, her resolve hardening. "You want a negotiation? It only happens on our terms."

He laughed, a low, mocking sound. "You're in no position to dictate terms."

Renée stepped forward, her anger grounding her. "And you're in no position to threaten us anymore."

Guzman looked at her with new interest, like a hunter re-evaluating his prey. "You've got fire in you," he said approvingly. "I like that." He tossed the envelope onto the table, its edges spilling secrets like blood from a wound. "Consider this a gesture of goodwill. Stay out of my business, and I'll stay out of yours."

James moved to cover it, but Nicole was faster, snatching it up. Her hands trembled as she opened it, revealing photos and documents she hadn't imagined existed—evidence of corruption and betrayal so deep it staggered her.

"You want me to believe this is real?" she demanded.

"What better way to destroy your enemy than from within?" Guzman replied, his voice silk over steel. "That's something James should understand very well."

James's jaw clenched at the barb, but he stayed silent, the weight of his betrayal heavy in the room. He felt Nicole slip further from him with every second, a chasm opening that he might never bridge.

Guzman moved towards the door, his exit as unchallenged as his entrance. "Think it over," he tossed back. "Just remember—I've already thought of everything." With that, he disappeared into the night, leaving a void filled with his cold, resonant laughter.

Nicole sank onto the couch, the envelope clutched tightly in her hands. Her world spun with too many revelations to catch hold of any one truth. Trust and deception twisted together like strands of barbed wire. She glanced at Renée, guilt piercing through her anger. "I brought this on us," she said, her voice raw.

Nicole's eyes met James's, fraught with both accusation and something unwillingly tender. "We've been in danger since you brought him into our lives."

James looked at her, his anguish laid bare. "And I've done everything I can to keep you safe. Even this."

Nicole's grip on the envelope tightened, the paper crumpling under her fingers. "Every decision you've made has been for you, not me."

Renée placed a steadying hand on Nicole's back, though her eyes remained fixed on James with a mixture of disbelief and fury. "We need time to figure this out," she said, her voice edged with finality. "Without you."

Nicole stood abruptly, shaking off Renée's comforting touch. Her decision was sudden but resolute. "I need time alone," she said, the words sharp and unexpected.

Renée blinked, a mix of confusion and heartbreak flashing across her face. "Nicole..."

But Nicole was already moving toward the door, her resolve unyielding. She couldn't look back, not now, not with everything so tangled and raw. "I have to figure this out," she insisted, her voice breaking as she left.

Renée's hands trembled where they had reached for Nicole, now helplessly suspended in the space she left behind. The shock of Nicole's departure hit almost as hard as James's betrayal. She turned to James, accusation boiling over into bitter words.

"She's leaving because of you," Renée spat, her composure finally splintering under the weight of all they had uncovered.

James opened his mouth to speak but found he had no defense, no explanation that could mend what he had

James flinched at the dismissal, his carefully constructed world crumbling around him. "If I leave, Guzman—"

"You've done enough," Renée cut in, her words laced with anger and heartbreak.

The room was a battlefield of wounded trust and exposed emotions as Renée led Nicole towards the door, putting distance between their fractured family and the man who had broken it.

James stood frozen, his desperation turning to a hollow resignation as he watched them go. Everything he had fought to protect slipped from his grasp like sand through his fingers.

Two weeks later, Nicole sat in her sparsely furnished apartment, the sterile newness of it a reminder of how much she had left behind. The television hummed in the background, a news anchor detailing the fallout from the evidence she'd turned over. High-profile arrests had rocked the city—senators, police chiefs, and executives—all charged with racketeering, kidnapping, murder, and bribery. The magnitude was staggering, but for Nicole, it was just another piece of the life she was still trying to reconstruct.

She glanced at her phone, anticipation and anxiety twisting in her gut. She had asked them both to come—James and Renée—and now she waited to deliver a decision that could break her all over again.

The doorbell rang like a gunshot in the silence. She took a deep breath and opened the door. Renée entered first, hesitantly, eyes searching for signs of where they stood. Nicole's heart ached with the memory of leaving her behind. James followed, his presence more subdued, yet still charged with unspoken desperation.

He looked worn, shadows haunting his eyes. "Nicole," he said softly, a world of unspoken questions hanging between them. They faced each other in an uneasy triangle, words stalled by the weight of what remained unsaid. Nicole took a breath, steeling herself for what had to come. "I wanted you both here because I've made a decision."

Renée's eyes widened, hope and fear warring in her expression. "Nicole, before you say anything—"

"No," Nicole interrupted, her voice firmer than she felt. "I need to do this before I lose my nerve." She paused, the enormity of it all settling over her like a shroud. "I can't keep running from what we had... but I can't go back to it either."

James winced at the finality in her tone. "You don't have to decide now," he said, desperation fraying his words. "I won't give up on us."

Renée shot him a hard glance but softened as she looked back at Nicole. "Whatever you decide, we'll make it work somehow."

Nicole's chest tightened with affection and frustration. "It's not just about us. It's about Noah too," she said, the mention of their son a fresh twist in the tangled knot of their lives.

"Everything has to change if we're going to keep him safe."

Silence enveloped them, thick with memories and possibilities. Nicole met Renée's eyes, the bond between them still strong but strained. "I want you both in his life, but I only need one partner in mine," she said quietly, each word a fragile step into unknown territory.

And I choose....

Epilogue

G uzman had underestimated their loyalty. He watched Nicole walk away, her steps quick and angry, and allowed himself a small, satisfied smile. The woman had fire, he'd give her that, but she was still just a woman. She'd believe what she wanted to believe, and what he'd given her was enough to plant doubt like a seed in her mind. James had switched the sperm—how could she trust him after that? The truth mattered less than the suggestion of betrayal. He knew enough about people to know that betrayal could do more damage than bullets.

He leaned back against the cracked leather of the town car, exhaling slowly. The deal with the Feds had cost him, but he'd given them just enough to satisfy them, just enough to buy himself some time. He could afford to lose a few small fish if it meant staying in the game. And Nicole? She'd stop writing about him, at least for now. He closed his eyes, feeling the wear of the last few weeks settle into his bones. For now, the pieces were coming together, and he welcomed the brief sense of control. The car turned a corner, and he let the movement rock him gently, a lullaby of power regained.

Guzman was already lighting a cigar when the wire slipped around his neck.

"Did you think you'd win, viejo?" The voice was low, and Guzman felt the breath of it against his ear, the pressure tightening, hot and sharp.

His driver's eyes were wide in the rearview mirror, frozen like a deer on the road. Guzman clawed at the wire, smoke spilling from his lips in ragged puffs as the cigar dropped to the floor.

"You made it easy," the voice continued, calm as a cat licking its paw. "Giving them all those names. Going soft for a woman."

The wire bit deeper, red seeping through Guzman's collar, and he felt the edges of his vision blur, everything narrowing to the pain and the voice and the knowledge that he had been wrong.

"Too bad I don't have my hammer. I'll take care of the family myself," El Martillo said, his tone almost tender.

Guzman's body twitched once, then stilled.

The driver watched, unmoving, as El Martillo loosened the wire, the tension all gone now, lifeless and limp. Guzman's head slumped forward, and the man who had been king of the streets slid to the floor like a marionette whose strings had been cut. The driver swallowed hard, fear slick in his throat.

"What now?" he croaked, eyes darting from the rearview to the road and back.

El Martillo took his time, straightening his shirt and settling into the seat as if he had always belonged there. "Now," he said, "we remind everyone who's in charge."